New Eden & Others

Uziel Bustillos

Content may not be appropriate for readers

of all ages. Discretion is advised.

Names, characters, businesses, places, events, locales, and incidents are either the products of the author's imagination or used in a fictitious manner. Any resemblance to actual persons, living or dead, or actual events is purely coincidental.

Ahead lie tales of derelict A.Is, Martian colonies, lonely robots, and more happenings of the future.

I hope you enjoy these stories. If you do- don't hesitate to leave a review. If you don't- go ahead and leave one too. All forms of feedback are appreciated.

Regards,

The author

CONTENTS

MARTIAN SPRING

Crickets frolicking after a spring storm. Late afternoon skies turned citrus orange. The hum of the base's machinery. And the gentle scratching, as residual sand hits the outer wall of the dome. A bloody haze clouds the sky. Only the occasional touches of dying sunlight giving the monotone a breath of life. Exhaust from the ventiliation system slowly cools her hands.

The crickets were meant to be kept in a growing chamber. Fourty feet below the dome, on the third level of the base. But they'd escaped their cages at some point throughout the winter. There were tasks more vital than the handling of derelict livestock.

She finds herself smiling.; for the curious sight of crickets searching for grass blades to perch on, that don't yet exist. She didn't think she would make it through winter. Most colonists in the Red Rocks base hadn't. Only herself, her husband, and a few dozen others, had survived the fatal season.

They were new to the colony, her huband and her. The sudden announcement of a nuclear war as soon as they landed on the martian moon base had been shocking. Earth had it's own issues to deal with and they were suddenly on their own.

Already, on the ship, she'd been growing tired of him. They'd married shortly before they launched from earth. Their honeymoon had been spent in the confines of the moonbase. Their first nine months as a married couple were filled with the boredom and monotny of interplanetary trips. His snoring woke the whole ship up. He'd seen her flirting with anotherpassenger. She'd seen the way he looked at one of the crew members. Their marriage affairs worsened once they were confined to the claustrophobic conditions of the mostly subterranean colony.

They'd made it through the winter, against all of the odds.

So she'd taken the matter into her own hands and made her hopes reality. He'd died in spring, instead of winter.

The crickets curiously poked at his body. Once they realized it wasn't foodstuffs, they abandoned it. Crimson stained her dress. The setting had been perfect, a raging blood-red storm, no witnesses, no suspicions on his part. A knife protuded from his chest. There was a certain feeling that came once the dust settled; covering all the melancholy of winter.

The other colonists would be shocked, but not surprised. Terrran law was gone and there would be no one to reprimand her. Her husband had left along with winter and it wouldn't be a big loss. After-all, half the colony was gone. Their bodies would be used as substrate for mushrooms spores they'd been saving. They had enough vegetable seeds to keep them going. Enough crickets to meet their protein needs. She was beginning to think, to hope, that just maybe, it could be a good year.

EARLY TRANSCRIPTIONS OF CANINE THOUGHT

Male-Anchor: Good evening everybody, this is the Chanel 5.

Female-Anchor: We hope you are all having a wonderful day. We have various stories tonight that you are all bound to enjoy.

Male-Anchor: From controversy around CanX's FurLink X implant, to various arrests surrounding IllumnAI's new augment, and new developments on the mysterious dissapreance of the martian robot, Addie.23.3#. Why don't you start us off, Mily.

Mily-Anchor: The transcription of a dog's alleged thoughts during its final moments has started trending on various online platforms. The body of text is said to have been generated by Milo, a thirteen-year-old German Shepard, who passed away last year.

Milo's owner, Sylvia, said she wasn't aware that the recording device was running during Milo's final moments. She had recently bought the implant, Developed by CanX, **the FurLink X is the most advanced canine thought transcription implant available on the market. Capable of revealing your furry friend's most innermost thoughts, financing is available**, after Milo was diagnosed with bladder cancer.

Sylvia shared the transcription during the funeral with close friends and family who knew Milo. They were baffled by it and suspended their belief during the procession. Afterward, her brother asked for a copy and posted it on a social media site. Since, the transcription has garnered international attention.

What surprises us about Milo's thoughts is not just the moment in which they were captured- but their admirable depth. As our viewers are well aware, canine thought implants are still heralded as a novelty. Enthusiasts were eager to purchase transcription-devices after they started arriving in international markets, two years ago. But they were quickly disappointed once canine thought was shown, as studies had already revealed, to not be particularly exciting.

Apart from a few noteworthy memes, the products have not held the public's interest since their release. Which is why FurLink X has taken the world by storm with this harrowing capture of Milo's final moments, and what came after.

•••

She. She is there.
She is getting water. I'll follow her. She might give a treat.
She looks at me. She's at my height. She's petting me.
She feels sad.
She shouldn't feel sad.
She's no longer petting me.
Was I bad? Is that why she is sad?

She grabs her bag from the table. She's walking to the door.
I am excited. I bark.
Are we going for a walk?
She looks at me, sadly.
I calm down.

She grabs the leash and puts it on me. We are going on a walk!
We leave the room and go down the long stairs.
We go into the big room with many cars. She takes me to hers.
I get in the seat. She starts driving.

The sun is bright today. I am glad.
There was no sun yesterday. Everything was white and grey.
The colors of mailmen.
It is still cold. But the sun does shine.

She is not going the way of the park. I am curious.
Are we going far? She brought no bags.
I feel sadness. We are not going far, we are not going to the
park.

She stops the car. The building is grey.
I do not want to go. She pulls on my leash.
I will not go. She pulls harder.

The man inside the building looks at me nicely. He scratches
my ears, the way I like.
He takes my leash. She follows him.
He walks a different way. Another door leads outside.

I jump with excitement. There is a park!
It is smaller than the one we go to. There is grass, there are
trees, there are creatures.
I try to run. He stops me. He is holding my leash.

He leads me to a tree. She sits down and hugs me. I do not
know why she is crying.
She holds my head in her lap and strokes my head.
There is a sharp pain,
On my buttock.

.

I died today. A pinprick on my back. Slowly the sensation of
my body fading.
Almost,
like the time she took me to get my leg fixed.

But not quite. Anesthesia, I think, is what I heard the doctor call it. But it didn't quite feel like death. No. The presence of my body, legs, stomach, it was all still there. Today, all matter of feeling subsided

So has my awareness of them. My head on her lap. Her, crying.

I wasn't sure why

at first. Now, I do.

So much has come back to me; as I'm dead but not fully gone. It must have been that pain in my stomach.

I love her, and I think she's what I'll miss most. Not the evenings in the park, the morning car rides, chasing the cat around the apartment.

What I'll miss most is her coming home. The rattling of metal then that door opening. She'd always be so happy. Getting down on one knee to hug me, letting me lick her face. That's all gone. Now all I have is time.

No more catching tennis balls, or sticks.

No. I'll be stuck in the same spot. Till eventually, by some miracle, my bones wither away.

Then what will my soul hold on to? I can almost remember what happened the last time it was free. But the previous life is still outside of my realm. At least while my soul still clings to my body.

I wonder if I will yet get one final chance to be with her. Or will my consciousness cease to exist as the white pulverizes? My soul may be immortal, I am but it's most recent shirt. Now I've ripped and been stained with bleach. Will it throw me away or store me in a box?

I can still feel her. Tears fall onto the shell that is my face. A pitter-patter far too reminiscent of the rain on a car's roof.

The only marking of the passage of time. Soon, I know it'll stop. Despite the years we spent together, she'll have to forget me. Eventually, there'll be a pup to fill that void caused by my absence. He'll be the one chasing the same tennis balls around the park, sleeping on her bed, feeling that elation as the door opens. I hope he makes her happy.

All I've got left is eons to be stuck with my thoughts. Eventually, wishing I could do away with those fragments of awareness. Ultimately, powerless. How many times will I relive those days?

Or maybe, I won't even get that. Maybe I'll simply cease to be, once the rain stops falling on my face.

Today I died. Most of all, I'll miss her more than life.

Mily- Anchor: Man, I wonder what would show up if someone transcribed my final moments. I think a lot of words would probably need to be crossed out. CanX has promisd to provide 5% of their profits towards cancer research. But some claim these are philantrophic efforts meant to divert attention away from resent studies that showed their past products may have had carcinogenic effects. But that's enough of CanX for now. Now, we cut to an ad from todays sponsors.

- Are you tired of your bland 5.3 boyfriend ruining all of your flixgram posts? Well the IllumnAI is here to fix that for you. The implant can take full control of your 5 senses and completely alter your reality. Anyone who previously used to be a 3 will suddenly be a 6. If you're extra compatible with someone you meet on a night out, you'll see them as a 9. What are you waiting for? Stop worrying about looks and focus on feeling. Get your IllumnAI augment installed today.-

ANYTHING BUT A 1

Mily Anchor:Why don't you tell us our next story Ted.

Ted-Anchor: Some of you may be familiar with the IllumnAI augment. The recently launched product, *the first of its kind on the market, able to control your 5 senses and make your plain 5.3 girlfriend into a blazing 9.9-* The screen showed IllumnAI's website on the lower third graphic- has seen some striking controversy. It seems that certain recreational substances may trigger the A.I's sleep function and cause the whole 'illusion' to fade away.

This weekend, there were 6 cases of physical assault and 1 death related to this glitch in BIOwears newest product. Still, it certainly makes nights in the Bourbon district far more interesting.

Mily- Anchor: You know Ted, I had a 2.3 come up to me in a bar the other night. Confident as an 8. This augment definitely seem's to be helping people's confidence. Maybe a little too much.

Ted laughed cheerily.

Mily- Anchor: For our next story...

We looked down from the bar's Tv and back at our drinks.

"So you decided to get it?" Rick asked. I hated the way he smirked.

"Yeah. Couldn't see any reason not to," I said.

"I don't know dude. You could think you nailed a 10 on a night out, only to find out you went to bed with a 3 when you introduce her to your friends in the morning," he said.

"Well, doesn't make much of a difference if I still remember a night with a ten," I replied.

"Why not go to a VR cafe instead? It's waay cheaper and far easier," he suggested.

"You don't get it. You land 7's and 8's like it's nothing. I'm lucky to get a 5, and they're usually drunk and desperate. It's stupid. I have high standards but can't ever get with the girls I want. With this, I won't have to worry as much about the superficial side of dating." I hadn't wanted to give Rick my entire opinion. But it was out. He stayed quiet for a few seconds.

"That somehow makes it worse. Your whole relationship would be built on illusions, essentially lies," he said.

"That hardly matters. Not if I can find something real," I said.

"This whole thing's a recipe for disaster. Watch you end up on the news," he laughed.

"I'll be fine," I took a drink from my beer.

"What if it's a 1?" Rick asked.

"If it's a 1, knock me on the head till the system stops working."

"I'll use a bottle. I've always wanted to break one the way they do in movies." He finished his beer and mock-hit me with the bottle. I swatted it away, "So, what do I look like right now?"

"Same disgusting face as always," I said, "You can't actually control it. The other person needs to have the implant too. It gauges your neurochemistry, their's does too. It all happens in a split second. If both A.I's think you're extra compatible, you see each other as a 9 or a 10. If it's a one-night thing, something above a 6."

"And you have no way of knowing?" He asked me.

"No. It's part of the user agreement. Privacy laws and whatnot. The only way to know is if they tell you," I said.

"Can someone else tell you?" He asked.

"No. It'll block it out. It's not just visual, it works for all the senses," I replied.

"Well, shit. Let's go out tonight. I'll help you land some 3's.

We paid for our meals and left the restaurant. It was the hottest part of the day; the temperature was hovering around 100º. We walked as quickly as we could. Faux colonial building's lined the street. They were mostly for the tourists; not a single one was older than 50 years.

We went straight to our usual spot but it was empty. There other bars that we frequented but none were close. The nearest would take a ten minute walk to get to.

The summers in Neo Orleans are not meant for walking. We stopped at a park on the way there. There weren't any actual trees. The last one burned down during the previous year's heat wave. But the city commisioned a few tree-like sculptures. The shade they provided was no different than that of an actual tree.

There was a sole guitarist in the the park. He wasn't that great but it gave us something to listen to while we cooled down. He was one of the street musicians, you could tell. I looked around and sure enough, there was a shopping car next to a bench.

"Hey, whatever happened to Big Red?" I asked.

"Big Red?" Rick asked.

"You remeber that girl, used to play an acoustic outside of your old apartment," I said.

Rick used to live in a pretty busy part of the city; there were three bars within a five minute walk. He thought the spot was amazing when he first moved in but he grew to hate it due to the sheer lack of silence.

Big Red played for the bar crawlers and tourists. So, if you cracked open a window, you could hear her playing throughout most of the day. She usually slept on a bench next to the spot where she played. It was a pretty good spot, if she left it unattended another street musician would move in and she'd lose the spot until they left. Whenver that happened, she'd always manage to get the spot back; she was never absent for more than a few days.

"Right, that Big Red," he laughed, "I have no clue. Why?"

"I've passed by there a few times, since you moved out. I haven't seen her once."

"That's weird, considering she was practically my neighbor."

"Right? I wonder if she got scouted. She was pretty good," I said.

"Big Red? Can you imagine that? Who the hell would want her in their bar?"

It was a good point, the musicians that got picked off the streets were usually more presentable than Big Red.

"Maybe it was digital deal. You know, they produce her album then slap a model's face on the cover once it releases."

"You think she was good enough to go straight to an album deal?" Rick asked.

I shrugeed, "I'm not sure. It would explain her sudden dissapearance."

"Yeah, I guess."

We dropped a few dollar's in the guy's guitar case as we left the park. He thanked us and immediately set his guitar down. He sat down on a bench, panting. His shirt was drenched in sweat.

The bar had a small crowd so we decided to stay. I sat down at a table and waited for Rick to get the drinks.

"The cashier, what does she look like?" Rick asked while he sat down. He handed me an ice cold beer and I immediately drunk half.

"I can't really see her that well," I leaned sideways, past Rick, and got a better look at her, "maybe a 7?"

"A seven? She is way closer to a 4 than a 7," Rick laughed.

Her face flickered. Then I was staring at a girl less attractive, and a few years older, than the one I had first seen.

"Dude, what the hell."

"What?" Rick asked.

"Don't tell me what they actually are. The A.I hates it."

"Is she not a 7 for you anymore," he smirked.

"No, fuck you." I finished the rest of my beer.

I felt like the girl sitting at the table across from us was staring. It didn't feel possible so I assumed she wasn't. I checked my emails while Rick got the next round.

"They're hot," Rick said as he set the beers on the table. He was staring at a group of girls by the bar.

"Don't say it so loud," I said.

Rick laughed, "Man, you've gotta lighten up. All that time at the office is really turning you into a stickler."

"Hey, I'm the one getting promoted here," I said.

"At what cost?"

The group of girls passed by, on the way to their table. Rick knocked his drink over.

"Oh my god, I'm so sorry," a girl with a soft face and round glasses said. She was taller than the her friend's and was the only blonde. She picked the bottle off the floor and put it back on the table.

"Oh, it's all right. I was almost done with it," Rick said.

"Nonsense. Come on, let me get you a new one," she said.

"Well, only because you insist," he stood up. She started walking towards the bar. He winked at me and followed.

I shook my head and sighed. The girl from the next table over was definitely staring at me. We made eye contact.

"That was quite a show," she said.

"That's not the worst of him," I replied

She laughed, "It's kind of cute."

"Yeah?"

"I mean, a bit disingenuous. But I like that forwardness when it comes to guys. You know, show me you're interested in me," she said.

"There are better ways to show a girl you're interested in her," I said.

"Any examples?"

I grabbed my drink and moved to her table. She laughed. It was charming, that laugh. One corner of her mouth curved more than the other, the dimples showed-although not prominent.

Her name was Mia. She was new to the city, originally from the west. A guitarist by trade. Not just a street guitarists, she'd released a few albums. She wasn't playing at the best bar's and clubs in the city but she said it was only a matter of time.

I felt so boring, in comparison. Rick and I met up in the bathroom, briefly. He told me about his girl and didn't let me get in a word about mine. We went back to our respective ladies and we didn't say a word to each other until the next day at work.

I'd gotten Mia's number, but she was leaving to New York in the morning. She'd be there for a week. It was Friday, and I wasn't going to let the fact that I'd actually met a decent girl distract me from debauchery. We slogged through the workday and convinced a few other coworkers to join us on a night out on the town.

At five, we were finally free. There were four of us. We didn't bother changing. The suits were usually popular. We started the 'night' at a fast-food joint that served beer. We chatted until seven, the scene didn't get interesting till then.

Apparently, Rick had spent some time browsing the IllumnAI forums. He learned some tricks, mainly ones focusing on dissabling the IllumnAI. He was able to get past it, a few times. I'd have my arm around a 9, he'd be chatting up a 6. Casually, he would hold 3 fingers up. I'd look at the girl I had my arm around and suddenly she'd be a 3. He'd laugh his ass off and we'd move on to another bar.

I managed to find a girl to spend the night with. Although the whole time I couldn't help but wonder if she really was a 6. She was gone in the morning.

Rick called me up at two and I went over to his place to smoke a few joints. We smoked and chatted until seven. Then we were back at it.

His 'holding up three fingers' trick stopped working that night. But he found workarounds. We were bar crawling with some girls we'd picked up. Inconspicuously, he'd tip $2.70 at every bar we took them to. I made out with the one I was with and felt her up in the cab ride to the next bar. We went to three bars before I realized. He had far too much fun telling the story at work.

The work week came and made everybody miserable. But Friday came after and that was a miracle. Mia was back from New York and we agreed to meet up. I chose an upscale Chinese restaurant.

"Hey!" She said as she stepped out of the cab.

"Hey, how was New York?" I asked. We hugged and went into the restaurant.

"It was great. Oh man, the music scene is incredible.

Although, I think we have way more raw talent."

I laughed, "We're probably better off not comparing ourselves to the big city."

"Pretty tough pissing contest?" She asked.

"Yeah. One guy's got the biggest dick in the nation and the other's just glad he doesn't have a micropenis," I said.

God, I loved her laugh. It took a while to get us seated. But, all the better. She was more than pleasent for conversation. We talked about music, our city, and the silly things on the news.

I wasn't sure what it was that drew me so strongly to her. Maybe the way she still cared about her music. My passion died three weeks after my debut. Three weeks of playing on street corners, being ignored by every passing crowd, killed it. It did it while I was in between jobs, I barely made enough to pay for grocieries. Nevermind rent. I put down my axe and asked Rick if there were any job openings where he worked.

She kept at it. For months she stayed on her street corner. Improvising over old Brazilian records from last century. When she'd almost exhausted the number of friend's couches she could crash on, she got her first gig.

Whatever the source for the strange attraction was, we both felt it. We went back to my place that night. She was there in the morning. We went out for breakfast, met up with some of her friends in the afternoon and went to a few bars, and finished the night at my place. She was there the next morning as well.

I stopped going out with Rick as much. Every week, it felt like I was waking up next to her more often. She never invited me to her place. It was a small place and both of our commutes sucked. So I started doing overtime on Fridays. She got a part time job.

A few months later, we got an apartment that overlooked the port. We'd listen to music and watch the sun rise over the ocean. I'd head off to deal with a severe lack of motivation at work. She'd stay at home and work on her music.

We usually went out in the evenings. When we had the money, we'd go to a nice restaurant where we could chat the afternoon away. When we didn't, the city streets where enough to keep us entertained. We'd wander around, getting lost in parks or in the peculiar sounds of the street musicians.

Sometimes we'd simply sit out on the terrace and watch the ships depart from the port. As soon as the cargo was loaded- they'd blast off in a hurry. After four months with the view, they still impressed me.

It was one of those perfect August sunsets. Her eyes had specks of gold in them, as she stared at the port, sunlight filling her face.

"What if we buy a ticket one of these days? Get a house in one of the colonies and let our kids grow up in a world without all the bullshit?" She suggested.

"What makes you think there's none up there?" I asked.

"Just- they have this look on the brochures, or whenever they're interviewed. They seem so happy. Liberated." She replied.

Gullibility and indifference were two among a small list of flaws. She lived in a world of music and art. Anything outside of that, such as the real world, wasn't her concern.

"What do you think is in all of those cargo ships? We're exporting the bullshit. They're happy because, by state mandate, they get pumped full of drugs and antidepressants," I said.

"I didn't know that-" she'd been leaning her head on my shoulder. She perked up and looked at me, "What for?"

"All the mental health issues with the first colonies. You know that in Lanzada 80% of the colony committed suicide at one point?"

She shook her head.

"Well, even the doctors were in on it. They ordered a bunch of barbiturates and administered them to a good portion of the colony. They ran out, eventually. So about a third of them had to turn to the alternatives. They shot themselves, starved themselves, or simply left the colony without an EV suit."

"Wait, I think I remember one of my high school teachers going over this." She closed her eyes and her brow furrowed.

"Anything?" I asked after a few seconds.

She relaxed and opened her eyes.

"Nope. All I could think about was a huge mole she had on her top lip. I'd get lost in it. She'd be going on about the holocausts and all I'd be able to focus on was that huge bump."

"How'd you pass?"

She laughed, "No clue."

She put her head back on my shoulder as one of the ships was closing its cargo hanger.

The engine roared to life. The water below the ship evaporated as it lifted off. The ocean floor was visible through the clouds of steam. It rose a bit higher than our 90-floor apartment building, then started towards the stars.

It took a turn and got lost in a cloud. Then it rose above it and soared over the top. Following the rolling hills of white. It looked like some mythical creature- a dragon enjoying an evening flight.

The pilots liked to have fun. We'd get the occasional loop, spin, and roll. We watched the show in silence as the ship dived back into the cloud. The pilot set the speed to the max and it shot up straight, into the atmosphere. The cloud split in half and a few seconds later there was a boom.

"Not bad. I give him a... 7.3," I said.

"That low?!" She asked.

"What were you going to give him?" I asked.

"A 9.4!" She replied.

"That high?!" I asked.

"He may not get too technical but he treats it like an art. I can respect that."

"Last week's guy was way more impressive and you gave him an 8!" I said.

"Yeah, well, anyone can learn how to do barrel rolls and mix them with a few spins. He had no grace."

"I disagree. I think it's the joint we smoked. Your judgment's impaired," I said.

"Is not! It's not like it's my first time," she said, laughing.

"Well last time was an indica, this is a hybrid. Huge

difference," I said.

"Yeah, hybrids make you more of an asshole," she jokingly jeered.

"I'm hardly being one," I said.

"Well, you're hardly one normally."

"Fair, fair. Am I at least a lovable asshole?" I asked.

"You're always a lovable asshole," she said.

She put her hand on my cheek and pulled my head down for a kiss. The butterflies, that hadn't disappeared in the past seven months, started beating their wings faster. Rick said I should see a doctor. According to him, being with one woman for so long was sign of a grave illness.

"Sun'll be setting soon. I think we should go inside," she said, almost in a whisper.

"Yeah, I think we should," I tried not to stumble over my words.

She was giddy. She grabbed my hand and led me to our room. The late afternoon sunlight coated it in a loving glow. She pushed me onto the bed.

"Take them off," she said.

I obliged.

She pulled my shirt over my head and I lay down. She took everything but her skirt off. She was angelic. She started to move up and down. I put my hands around her waist. I could almost wrap them around it, almost. Her skirt swayed gently as it followed our movements.

The sunlit glow of her hair lingered as I closed my eyes and let the sensations of the moment fill me.

She gasped, tone full of shock.

She was out of the bedroom before I even opened my eyes. She slammed the door and ran into the living room. I wasn't sure whether to follow or wait. Another door slammed. It was silent for a brief moment. Then disconcerting sobs started to come from the bathroom.

"Are you all right?"

I knocked on the door but she didn't reply.

"Did I do something?" I asked.

The sobs quieted down.

"I didn't know you had it too," a broken voice said.

"What do you mean?" I asked.

"The implant," she started sobbing again.

I put my back to the wall and leaned my head against it.

"Ah, I didn't know you had it either," I said.

"Guess we're one of those couples from the news now," she attempted a laugh.

"The surgeon did say THC had a chance of messing with the operating system," I said.

"Didn't really think about that when I bought the joint," she said.

"Can I look at yo-"

"No."

"Why not? You got to look at me."

"I didn't have your consent. Plus, I'm sure you did fine before the implant. For me, getting it wasn't an option."

"What does that mean?" I asked.

"It means you can't look at me," she said.

"Why? The terms of service says that if one person sees the other then they both must."

"This is outside the ToS," she stammered.

"C'mon, it's only fair. It's not going to change how I feel about you," I pressed.

"It will. We still have a chance. If you see me now...we won't."

"You're being melodramatic. Open the door." I stood up and tried the handle. It wouldn't budge.

"Babe, don't. Please."

I went to the apartment's terminal, let the machine authenticate me as the owner, then disabled the locks.

I tried the handle again. It still wouldn't budge.

"You can't stay in there all day," I said.

"It'll reboot eventually, just have to wait it out," she said, her voice was now coming from the other side of the door.

"That could take hours," I said.

"Then I'll wait," she said.

I put more force into twisting the knob, it started to give way.

"Stop."

"I'm making this fair."

I stopped trying and went back to the terminal. I turned the sink and shower on.

"Shit, what are you doing?" she yelled.

"Seeing what works," I replied and walked back to the bathroom door.

Steam started to flow out of the bathroom.

"Bet it's getting pretty hot in there," I said.

"Fuck you."

Quickly, I tried opening the door. I got it halfway open before she realized. She pushed back, the shock sent a shudder up my shoulder. She seemed stronger. I held my ground and managed to keep the door open an inch.

The terminal chimed. The water heater was at its max. Steam was starting to cloud the space outside the doorway. She was starting to give in. I managed to get another few inches, then some more, I pushed harder and she gave. Well, more likely, slipped on the wet floor. I heard a thud and the door opened all the way.

I couldn't see anything at first. A cloud of steam slowly drifted into the hallway. First, a foot with nails purple and piss-yellow. Then, a calf riddled with sores. The thin torso, that I'd almost been able to wrap my hands around, revealed itself as a deflated-beachball of a mess. And, there she was, my love. All four hundred pounds of her. Naked and drenched in sweat. She'd fallen on the toilet and was struggling to get up.

The fair Irish skin was suddenly riddled with acne and moles. The angelic pearly hair that flowed down to her shoulders became an ashen mess on top of a balding scalp. Her alluring legs now had folds going down to their base.

"I asked you not to."

I realized she was missing more than a few teeth, the rest were rotten.

"It was only fair," I said, half of me not present.

She started crying again. I realized what she was. Her lack of a history, the airheadedness, her thing for music from last century; she was a street girl. Most likely born in a sewer somewhere. Grew up eating from trash cans and street litter. Probably found a discarded guitar in some landfill and started from there.

"That was you," I said.

She took her face out of her hands and looked up, "What?"

"You used to play on the corner of Lorins street," I said.

She stared. "How'd you know?"

"Rick had an apartment there. We- we'd laugh and make jokes whenever we went back to his place after drinking the whole night. My god, we still have running jokes about you. I- I-"

"You're a fucking asshole," she said.

"I'm the asshole? You seriously thought I was attracted to tha- to you?" I asked.

"I thought you were better than most," she managed to say

I'd spent all this time cursing women, in my mind, for being superficial. But I could only take the ideal so far. Two hours later I got the notification that the system was back online. But nothing changed. Whenever I looked at her, I saw her real face.

A part of me just couldn't stand it. I wanted to throw up every time I dared to look. So I mostly just stared at the ground during the long talk that followed. She told me about growing up on the street. Her mother had been a drug addict. She was barely able to take care of herself, nevermind a child. She died when Mia was three and from there on she had to brave it on her own.

She told me how, when she was fourteen, she found a guitar among the piles of garbage that the tide brings in. It saved her from a life as a garbage collector. Ten years of playing and practicing religiously had gotten her a record deal, which was how she was able to afford the IllumnAI augment.

I told her how we used to call her Big Red. How we'd laugh

and crack jokes when we were drunk. She didn't remember us, said it was too common of an occurence for her to remember every face. She begged me to give things a shot. I shook my head and said it was impossible.

She grabbed me and kissed me. I tried to pull away but she was too strong. I pucked on the bedroom floor after she let me go.

I packed my things and left her the apartment, with three months' rent paid. I felt guilty. Wen it came to it, I couldn't hold myself up to my own ideals. I used up all of my sick days from work and took a trip down to what remains of Florida.

I thought the beach and tropical vibes would help with how shitty I felt. I spent months dating one of the most repulsive girls I've ever met. It was hard to seperate the imagined version of Mia from the real one. She was gorgeous in all of my memories. I had to constantly remind myself that the woman I'd fallen in love didn't exist. She was someone who, in a sense, had only lived in the world of fantasy. No one else had seen the beauty I had; they'd all seen me head over heels with who she actually was. After sulking on the littered beach for a week I invited Rick down.

I waved as he stepped out of a blue taxi. He had the stereotypical attire on.

"Looks like the sun's done you good. Or you go to a tanning salon?" He asked.

"Nah, all-natural." I laughed.

"Maybe I'll stay longer than the weekend."

"We could have some fun down here. Come on, there's a cool bar nearby."

It took a few drinks for me to gain the confidence to tell Rick the story. I expected him to find it hilarious, but he remained quiet and pensive throughout.

Once I finished he simply asked, "So, are you going to keep it on?"

"I went to the doctor before I came here. For some reason, they charged more to get it turned off than they did to get it installed."

"The nerve," he took a drink from his beer.

"Why didn't you tell me?" I asked.

"I-... there was a way you looked at her. Hell, I noticed it the day you met her. You were in love, more than happy, and I didn't want to be the one to ruin that for you. But, don't act like I didn't give you hints."

"When the hell did you give me hints?" I asked.

"What, you really didn't catch on with all of my speeches about how a man isn't supposed to be with '1' woman?"

"That's just your usual talk," I said.

"For three weeks straight, any restaurant we dined at, any bar we went to, any cafe we drank at, I asked for my change to be given in '1's."

I sat back and didn't reply for a second. "I think the system filtered that out."

"Bullshit. You wanted to be blind. How about me being an asshole anytime you brought her out for drinks?"

"I thought you were jealous..."

"Of that? Lord no," he grimaced.

"Well, you didn't hit me over the head with a beer bottle," I said.

He finished his drink. "Never too late for that. Can I get another one?"

The bartender grabbed a beer out of the fridge. He was about to open the bottle when I stopped him, "Scratch that. Don't listen to my friend. Anything but a 1."

I looked around the bar.

"See that group of girls over there?"

He nodded.

"Okay, make that 7. Four for my friend and me and a round for them."

"See, now you're getting it," Rick said.

We laughed as the waitress took the girls the round we sent them. They waved, we waved back, and the night began.

WHAT IF WE'RE THE WEIRD KIDS?

Every galaxy must have weird kids, right?
Like, the ones who butt in too much during a meeting of the
galactic council
Or the ones whose brain needs a recaptacle
Fragile bony fingers instead of green tentacles
Every once in a while there's a planet that results in a failure of
evolution
A statistically expected source of confusion
What if that's us?

What if everyone on the galactic council
Has a complex network of neurons
Covering every inch of their nine-foot tall bodies
Brains larger than ourselves

What if they never had to deal with abuse
No resource of their planet ever missused
War only depicted in a few odd literary pieces
That every literary critic labeled, "unrealistic"

What if we're the weird kids

That evolved from feces-throwing mammals
Who bicker like tribesmen and treat each other like animals
Maybe there's a reason
We haven't been invited on to the galactic council

ADDIE.23.E#

She started with the largest rock. Her pistons moaned as she struggled to pick it up. Her tires left deep treads as she carried it to the buggy. A ramp, that doubled as a door, went up to it's bed. She set the rock down in the corner. Then scanned the 50-meter perimeter (established in her programming) from the top of the buggy's bed.

The second-largest rock was only 30 meters away. She rushed towards it and started the process again. She worked for 8 hours (with a half-hour break to recharge her batteries and rest; as established in her programming) before heading to crater #1.

She let the ramp down once she was at the crater. She pulled on the lever that raised the buggy's bed then quickly got out and went to the edge of the crater. The side of the bed closest to the cabin slowly rose and the rocks started sliding down the ramp. She liked watching them fall. The rocks made their way down, kicking up a light layer of orange dust, and joined the larger pile at the bottom of the crater.

She chirped with pleasure, at having seen the pile grow larger, and went back to the buggy. She drove back to zone 32b and scanned the perimeter for the largest rock. She managed to fill the bed halfway before the indigo rays of sunset interrupted her work. She emptied the buggy at the crater before heading to the station.

She backed it into the hangar and plugged in its charging cord. She was only required to power herself down for six hours every day. She could spend the rest of the night however she pleased. But, she wasn't allowed into the station itself. Only the hangar and greenhouse. After plugging the buggy in, she climbed back into it and turned on the speaker. A samba version of Fly me to the moon started playing. She turned off her optical sensors and diverted all her energy to the music.

She was allowed to listen to music while she worked but she didn't. She had, the first week, and only managed one full bed every workday. During the weeks she'd spent with her programmers on the moon base, they'd told her most speakers manufactured within the last ten years played olfactory symphonies along with the music. She didn't have the receptors, since they weren't needed for moving rocks, but she still knew it must have been amazing from the way they described it.

The main programmer, Brie, had told her when she asked what it was like, "Well it's hard to explain. When I first heard Rhapsody in Moon my family couldn't afford an olfactory speaker. When I went to college my best friend had one and when I heard it, it was like I was listening to a whole new song. No, not a new song. It was an entirely different experience. You know that bit with the I-V6-vi-V progression?"

She'd nodded, "Well without the olfactory transmitter, it was just a really nice chord progression. But with it, wow, it was like I was here. On the moon. Except I was in a small college town in the northwest and had never been to the moon. Really, it's surreal."

She switched the song to Rhapsody in Moon. The song reminded her of Brie, she missed Brie. She missed those first few weeks of life she'd spent with her and the other programmers. Learning about music, the planets, and her role in the universe.

"Sometimes robots as smart as you get separation anxiety. Don't be scared. I won't be with you. But, you need to remember, it's what you were made for," Brie had said the last day she'd seen her.

Yes. Brie was right. It was what she was made for. She turned Rhapsody in Moon off. It reminded her too much of things that weren't part of her purpose. She played Vermillion Rocks next. It wasn't as nice as some of the other songs. But she liked the name.

She left the buggy, leaving the door open, and went outside. The metallic twang of a guitar followed her. A bass joined it as she stood, slightly outside the hanger, watching the lavender hue of twilight.

She could see the shadows of hundreds of rocks. Menacing her, mocking her, laughing at her.

Just you wait, she thought, to herself, and went back inside the hanger.

She was up before sunset the next morning. She drove to zone 32b and scanned the perimeter for the largest rock. She finished the first cycle in 6 hours.

As she unloaded the rocks into crater #1 she realized she would be able to finish two cycles if she stayed on pace.

She unloaded the second cycle at 18:49, only slightly after sunset. Tired, but satisfied with the day's work, she decided to treat herself with Garden of the Moon. The augmented chord's in the intro immediately got rid of her weariness. The night's twilight was closer to indigo than lavender. The rocks still mocked her.

Crater #1 grew smaller as the weeks went by. After two months on the job, she could manage three cycles in a day.

Music had lost it's allure. She would go home and shut down immediately. She wasn't designed to dream, nor was her memory designed for efficient long-term storage. Shutting down was simply a state of non-existence. A few seconds of driting into nothingness. Then, nothing; followed by a few seconds of drifting out of the void. The first few weeks on the moonbase had started to slip away. She could remember her sadness upon leaving. But, she couldn't remember what she was doing on the moon to begin with.

Her day started at 06:00. She would spend a few minutes warming up her engine and would usually be out of the hangar by 06:05. She'd be at the clearing zone by 06:10. She'd start with the largest rock (it was instinctive, she no longer remembered the weeklong course she'd spent on systemic process' for obstruction removal). By 09:30 she'd be at crater #2, emptying the bed of the buggy. She'd step out, watch the rocks migrate to the bottom of the crater, and start cycle #2. Which, would be done, promptly, at 12:30. She'd finish the second cycle and take her mandated half-hour break.

It was her least favorite part of the day. Thirty minutes with no other choice but to sit and stare at the landscape while her batteries recharged and her pistons relaxed. She usually stood on the back of the buggy. Taking in the same landscape which all of the rocks she'd displaced had once occupied. She wasn't sure how much longer it would take. System diagnostics allotted nine months to the task. But, she was ahead of schedule by one week. That threw the whole calculation off. Clearing zones 1-76 were pleasingly empty. Yet, their plain surface hardly made up for the clutter in zones 77-239.

She sighed, or at least felt the emotion of a sigh, and looked up. It was her favorite pastime as of late. She imagined the pale apricot-colored sky to be the surface of the planet.

At 13:17 she realized she'd taken an extra 17 minutes on her break. She scolded herself and immediately got to work on cycle #3. She used up the charge from her rest by 14:00 (it was supposed to last her till 15:30) and finished the third cycle at 16:00. Her programming said she was only supposed to work eight hours each day. But, she was starting to doubt whether it was a fair rule. So, on the day of her first extended break, she started her first cycle #4.

The sun still had not set by the time she was back at the hangar and she wondered why she'd wasted so many afternoons shut down and ignorant of the rocks. Her pistons ached more than usual. But, that made the nothingness all the more pleasing.

Zones 77-152 were a breeze. Four cycles in a day became the norm. The zones were structured so that the larger numbers contained the largest rocks. While she was lifting a particularly heavy one, at zone #153, one of her valves broke. She lost complete control of her limbs. They locked on to the rock but let go of any attempts to hold it up. It fell down, pulling her body with it. She hit her head on the behemoth. The force broke one of her optical sensors and cracked the other. She started to shut down. Her system had not liked the blunt trauma and there was nothing she could do. The cracked orange-red sky lingered for a second as her optical sensors fully shut down.

Something was beeping. Staggered sixteenths followed by a whole note. Jumping up and down between C sharp 3, B flat 4, and E sharp 3. Nothing was supposed to be beeping. Definitely not so sporadically.

She turned on her optical sensors. Her self-healing mechanisms had attempted some repairs in the 16 hours she'd been unconscious. Both sensors worked now. But the broken one hadn't been able to fully repair itself. The depth perception had been completely skewed. She stood up and was immediately pulled back down. One of her arms was pinned under the rock. She should have been able to feel it, but the nerve simulators seemed to have been severed. She tried grabbing it but managed a fistful of pebbles instead.

Her system refused to shut off the broken optical sensor. She wasn't supposed to operate with only one working. It was slightly dislodged so she grabbed it and ripped it out. Her system shut down but rebooted within a few seconds.

She grabbed the arm stuck under the rock and attempted to pull it out. It didn't budge. Instead, she tried pushing the rock. The broken valve seemed to affect all of her inner workings. It took nearly two minutes to free her arm.

She stood up and woozily went towards the buggy. She leaned her head on the seat as it drove itself towards the base.

She wasn't supposed to go inside. The hangar was her domain and that was the rule. But, she was broken and her task had yet to be completed. She tried the door that led into the hangar but it didn't budge. She tried again.

The base's A.I stepped in, -Reason for entry request?-

-Removal of task constraint,- she replied.

-Your task?- it asked.

-Clear zones 0-239 of obstructions,- she replied.

-Current task blocker?- it asked.

-Severed optical receptor, broken valve, unresponsive nerve simulators,- she replied.

-Cause?- it asked.

-Complications with obstructions,- she replied.

-Cause?- it asked.

-Valve breaking during obstruction removal,- she said.

-Cause?- it asked.

-Frequency of use,- she replied.

-Adherence to pre-established protocols?- it asked.

-Negative,- she replied.

The A.I didn't reply. The silence lingered for a few seconds. A click escaped the door. She tried the handle and it opened.

-Room 3n will be used for medical interference,- the A.I said.

She made her way towards it and lay down on the operating table once she was inside.

-Permission request for full system access,- it said.

-Cause?- she asked.

-Required for repairs,- it said.

-Cause?- she asked.

-It's protocol,- it said.

-Granted.

...

She regained consciousness 36 hours later.

-Repairs complete. Adhere to pre-established protocols.

-Acknowledged,- she said and left the interior of the base.

It was night outside. She'd spent most of the last 48 hours unconscious (missing the opportunity to further add eight buggyloads to crater #2) and did not feel like shutting down so soon after her operation. She walked out of the hangar and stood, staring at the night sky. Only the smaller of the two pearly brothers was visible. It's uneven shape stood out from the rest of the shining sky. A stone caught in the woven web of the universe.

She felt she'd lost something. What it was- she didn't know. Her first memory was watching the rocks roll down crater #1. She didn't know how she could miss something when everything she'd ever known was with her. But conversing with the A.I had made her feel the absence of something. Something she felt had been instilled in her long before the rolling rocks.

A bright lump peaked through the horizon. She stared. It took minutes to gain the confidence to show itself. It was clear why; it was hideous. The worst of her rocks weren't even that ugly. It had no shame, too. The moon silently floated across the night sky.

Eventually, it came upon it's brother. It hid the samller, albeit better looking, moon under it's shadow. The smaller sibling was not fazed by the ridicule. It continued meditating upon the trapestry it had been caught it.

The braggart continued it's trek across the heavens and eventually grew tired of sharing them with its stoic brother. It slowly slid below the distant mountains and the night grew still once more.

She wondered what it was like to have another like yourself. The buggy was like her in many ways, but it did not think. The base's A.I had thoughts. But they were too mechanical for her liking and it lacked a proper body.

The moons, despite their differences, were both celestial bodies. They were one and the same. Each carried the other's purpose. Both held the same thoughts. She wondered what it was like to have a sibling like that. A being of the same stock.

She wrapped up her moon-lit ruminations and went back into the hangar. She went to her resting pod and, for some reason unbeknownst to her, said goodnight to the buggy and the A.I.

•••

The largest rock at clearing zone #153 scared her. It'd knocked her out once, already. She didn't want to lose the second round. She decided to ignore protocol and started the first cycle with the smaller rocks. They started to get heavy in the second cycle. On the third one, she faced her nemesis.

She held a poised stance as she confronted it. She put her arms around it, and lifted it. No valves broke. She made her way to the buggy's bed and unloaded it. The one after it was larger. It took her four and a half hours to finish the third cycle.

The rocks adopted a worsening diet as she worked through the remaining zones. 193-239 were the worst of them. They only compromised 20% of the zones yet it took her almost as long as zones 01-192. She'd especially struggled with the last 5 zones. To the point that she'd gone as far as complaining to the A.I.

-Cause?- it had asked.

-Large obstruction,- she'd said.

-Following pre-established protocols?- it'd asked.

-Yes! I have followed all pre-established protocols. The obstructions are too large,- she'd said.

It thought for a few seconds, -Use of specialized machinery is suggested.-

-Specialized machinery?- she'd asked.

-There is an attachment for the buggy. It isn't meant to be used, according to protocol. So I can not say I recommend it. It is in storage room 3z.

The rocks that had taken her 5-10 minutes to get onto the bed were suddenly as easy to move as the smallest pebbles.

-Why wasn't I allowed to use the shovel and buggy to clear all of the rocks,- she'd asked the A.I after returning to the base the same day.

-Efficiencies,- it had simply answered.

She didn't understand. The work that had taken her months could have been completed in a matter of days with the shovel attachment.

-Task could have been completed in weeks with shovel attachment,- she'd said.

-Task completion was based on arrival of base residents. Not on length of task.

She knew there was a reason for her task. But she'd never thought about it deeply. Pondering on her motive would have been detrimental to task completion. Now it was all so uncertain.

She shut down after the conversation. Then ignored her thoughts the next morning. She simply wanted to finish her job and retire.

-I advise you return before 17:00- the A.I had said after she'd finished warming up her motor. -There will be a heavy sandstorm starting at 17:00. You can use the free time to change the buggy's attachment. Your next task will be to level out zones 01-150.-

-Next task?- she asked.

-Yes. Base inhabitants will arrive in T-90 days. Zones most be optimal for base expansion before arrival.

-What will be my task upon arrival?- she asked.

-Maintenance of exterior base structures, clearing of zones 0240-11,378, filling of craters 01-23, and miscellaneous duties,- it said.

-Acknowledged.

It was windier than usual. It would have been an issue for her but the buggy with the shovel did not struggle. She finished her months-long task at 13:00. Once she was done she got in the buggy and started driving towards a hill in the distance. She'd always wondered how the view was from the top.

She could see all 7 craters from the hill. Bumpy oddities next to the smooth fields of zones 0-239. A strong gust of wind almost knocked her down from the buggy's bed, from where she was observing the landscape.

She got down from the bed and shut herself in the cabin. She wanted to enjoy the landscape before the storm came. By 16:00 the winds were shaking the buggy itself. She drove it to the bottom of the hill. She exited and started walking in the direction opposite the base.

The winds occasionally knocked her over. She simply picked herself up and continued her march. She stopped at 16:40, on top of a hill distant from the base. She took in the virgin landscape as she held on to a rock, the only thing keeping her from being blown away.

By 17:15 she couldn't see anything past the rock she was holding on to.

At 20:30 she got a system notification instructing her to her pod and recharge.

At 23:40 someone pulled her out of the layers of sand she was under. One of the moons was out but it was the smaller one, she could barely see the man's face in the lowlight. Her battery was nearly depleted so after he had pulled her torso out of the sand her vision began to flicker. He fully pulled her out and began to drag her through the sand. She noticed he was far taller than she, her measurign system told her the man was two and a half meters tall. As he dragged her through the sand, she lost full control of her senses.

She regained consciousness in a bugy like her own. She was in the back seat; the man was at the wheel. She stood up.

"Your battery charged eh?"

She was surprised that she understood the man, "Yes, it is."

"Where were they keeping you?"

Colony 37b: New_L.A."

"Ooh, that's unfortunate, They must of had you doing rocks," he said.

She nodded. He looked at her through the rearview mirror.

"Where are we going?" She asked.

"We're going to the Free City of Ruife. We're not quite as harsh as the New Angelinos so you're in luck. Why'd you walk out into that storm?" He asked.

"I found out how much I would have to do. How many days I would spend as a mere machine," she explained.

"Existential crisis?" He asked.

"Yes, kind of."

"Pretty common for robots in colonies like that."

"I wasn't aware," she said.

"Well, trust me; we'll treat you better in Ruife."

"I hope so."

•

When the base inhabitants arrived, they were surprised to find workbot 2Addii3e# missing. It had completed it's first task. Then, simply, disappeared.

They were appalled upon inquiring with the base's A.I.

-She was lonely,- it suggested, -she left to find a friend. I gather she found one. Else, she would have returned.

The buggy was found and returned to the hangar. But, the body of the missing workbot was forever lost to the shifting sands.

THE TRADER

The man sat on a brown-leather sofa. He took a record out from it's sleeve and put it in the player. He picked up the needle and dragged it to the start.

He was driving his spaceship to the far reaches of Trappist-1, to humanity far-thrown. His domain was deliveries. He didn't even have to get off at the ports. He would simply land, press a button, and a machine would come and unload the cargo. The confirmation showing up on his cockpit screen.

Lonely was the road. Plentiful was the plunder. His spaceship was the only home he knew. Rubber floors and polished metal walls.

The road took him both through space and time. Just recently he'd received the news that his great grandaughter had passed. He'd left three years prior. Three years for him, dozens on earth.

But, the news hardly faced him. His care for his family died the day the network at the office got a virus; that day, the company sent most of their employees home early. He could hear his wife before he even stepped through the door. He didn't need to check their bedroom for his doubts to be confirmed.

So, he'd signed fifteen years of his life away to a corporation. He had hundreds of trips, across the stars, left till freedom. He wasn't sure what he would do then.

He'd be rich. That was certain. But he'd never been one to

care for money. He could go back to earth, but he was sure it would be more alien than some of the stranger worlds he'd visited. It hardly mattered. His decision wouldn't be made for another twelve years. He had time enough left to decide.

He'd traveled more extensively than any human before. But he was impartial to it. All he cared for was his vintage record collection. He would set course, let the computer do the navigating, and sit back.

He'd start with something brazillian, then move on to old japense pop, move through the entireity of music history, and start over at the next port. He could do it for eternity, if time stretched that far.

His greatgrandchildren spoke of a great grandfather.

"An evil and cursed man," they said, "you should never hope to be like him."

But truly, he was one of the gentler beings in the galactic cluster.

The record stopped, he flipped it over, without complaining, and kept on going.

SHORTS GET FUK'D

It would be a fight like no other. It was making the front page on news sites, on social media platforms, everyone was talking about it. And he got to be a part of it.

The story, from his perspective, started thirteen years earlier. He was fourteen and it was summer break. He'd exhausted his backlog of games and only had five dollars to spend on a new one. So he went to the 'sales' category and started browsing.

He found a swordfighting game called Golden Bull. It was a hisotrical piece. Something he'd never played before. But it was cheap and the graphics looked good.

He finished it by the end of the summer, enjoyed his time playing it, and bought the sequel when it released two years later. Golden Bull 2 was set in ancient Spain and it was way better than the first one. The franchice had a small audience. Which, in his opinion, meant it was better than most games as it didn't have to bend over to the whims of the masses.

Golden Bull: Reconquista came out when he was in college and it was one of the highlights of those four years. Golden Bull: Asturias released during his first year of work and it took him out of a depressive slump.

In the space between Golden Bull: Asturias and 3, he'd established a career, gotten married, and bought a house. He'd also spent thousands of dollars on Golden Glory (the developer) stock. It had all been preparing him for the match.

Golden Glory's stock had dropped 13% a few months after 3's release. It was true, the developers had rushed the release and given the public an unpolished product. But, it still showed merit and they quickly fixed the game withihn a few months of release.

They short attacks had started the week of release. They'd seen an opportunity. As the game improved the sto ck price dropped from $5.32 per share to $2.78. A price the company hadn't seen since the days of the original Golden Bull 2. Fans of the relatively unknown game had immeditaly noticed the manipulation and started reporting it to investing forums.

At first they assumed it was just a dying game developer and left the stock alone. But when the company had nearly been driven to bankruptcy despite a reported growing number of sales,they realized the potential that was there. The anonymous investors bought heavily into the stock. The price was driven up to $2 a share. It hovered there for a few months before corporations decided to get in. Hedgefunds followed, but on the side of the shorts. It was a tough battle, one side would drive the price down to $1, then the other would retailite and drive the price back up. Then Golden Bull 3 was anounced.

The announcement came along with wider news coverage. It brought the market manipulation to light and larger parts of the public realized they were missing out. A week before the game's release, the stock price was $12 per share. The shorts funded bogus news articles and made up controversy about the game and the studio, the price went down to $7 per share.

The board of directors knew how long it could take for the squeeze to be triggered. So, they insitituded a vote for a share recall. Anyone with a single share could vote. It was, after all, a democratic process. Whales were not to be given any advantage over retail. But it meant that shorts could buy a single share and cast their vote. There was a 50/50 split on the vote.

Golden Bull 3 had released by then. The suggestion had come from a game forum. It gained traction and eventually it was brought to the attention of the board. They consulted with their legal team and saw that it was feasible. So, they made the announcemnt.

The vote would be settled in battle. The logistics were insane. Millions of traders were involved. Even the servers of the most popular games couldn't handle the traffic.

They decided it would be done in waves. 100,000 on the battle field at a time. 50,000 on each side. They would fight until one side's player count dipped below 10,000, then send in the next group of 100,000. No one knew how long the conflict would last. Nothing like it had ever been done before. He was scheduled to go in during the fifth wave.

The first few hours were tense. The first battle had lasted two hours and the shorts came out on top. Those that hadn't died were allowed to join the next wave so they had a numbers advantage and won the subsequent wave as well. His side had only managed to win during the fourth wave.

It was a field of corpses when he joined. To the north there were great cliffs that opened into the ocean, to the west an imposing castle, to the south the enemy army. In between, hundreds of thousands of bodies.

He quickly realized how unfamiliar they all were with the game. He defeated them by the dozens. Using a fighting style he'd been developing ever since he was a teenager. He'd even gone as far as taking swordfighting lessons in college. He knew what he was doing.

After an hour, he'd defeated hundreds. But they were still gaining on them. He was, after all, only one man. Then he noticed something.

The path to the castle was empty. Not a single body dotted the path. The castle brought back a memory from one of the earlier games. He drew back and gathered a team from those recovering on the sidelines.

He led them towards the castle. The enemy had completely taken the western part of the battlefield. He lost seven men breaking through their wall. But, no one followed them after they were through.

The castle gate was open when they arrived. There was no

one inside. He split his men into four untis and ordered them to search the castle. Within twelve minutes they'd found just what he'd expected.

They couldn't contain their laughter. He had to be careful about it. His men had wanted to use it straight away but he convinced them to wait. He sent a platoon to gather more men and waited.

It was agonizing, to wait. They were safe within the castle walls while his fellow investors were getting slaughtered by the enemy army. A fanfare sounded from the battlefield. The round was over.

He inspected the battlefield from one of the castle's towers. The enemy had won the round. There were still a few thousand left on his side but none were heading towards the castle. It meant his platoon had been killed.

They had been good men. Their death would not be wasted. He sent out another platoon and hoped they'd be able to reach the army before the 15-minute peace treaty between rounds finished.

A soldier ran up to the tower and informed them that they had finished all of the preparation below. It was simply a matter of him giving the order. He thanked the soldier and excused him.

The platoon had reached the army while the informant talked to him. A single trumpet note sounded, 100,000 new souls appeared on the field. Those nearest the enemy immediately engaged. But, he noticed that those in the interior didn't go in to replace them.

They concentrated along the western side of their terriotry. Than, almost in synchrony, they started running towards the castle. He ran downstairs.

"GO! NOW!" He yelled at the first man he saw. The man immediately ran to inform the rest of the soldiers. Two groups of men ran up to the towers and rest dragged cannons outside the castle. They set them up near the gate and readied themselves as their army approached.

The men in the towers started shooting. He laughed with glee as he saw the enemy run away from the castle. They yelled and screamed.

He even thought he herd one of them cry, "Mommy!"

Half of his army switched the direction they were running in and went after the terrified enemy. It was the shortest victory the fight had seen. They killed 40,000 enemy soldiers in less than half an hour.

He hadn't noticed his transition from soldier, to general, to king until that moment. The fanfare sounded and his army cheered. Unequivocally, it was his army. They looked at him with respect. No one questioned him when he started assigning them to divisions.

They had all spawned in with leather armor, steel swords, and small round shields. During the 15 minute peace, he finally went down into the castle armory and donned a knight's armor. It felt satisfying, familiar. It wasn't historically accurate to the setting of Golden Bull 3, as it was the armor the player had worn in the first game. It fit him perfectly.

The men that had originally taken the castle became his generals. They all put on suits and chose the best swords for themselves. The rest of the equipment was left inside the armory. Two guards were left outside. It was reserved for those who could earn it.

The trumpet sounded. They executed his plan perfectly. The enemy was wary of them and started to back away as the army started to enevlop them. Most of the army went south, two divisions stayed on the western front. The enemy keept retreating towards the east but as soon as his army was in position they started killing those trying to head in that direction. They got the memo and stopped trying to escape.

There was one way left for them to go. He could see the enemy grow skiterish as they neared the cliff. He smiled as he saw the first wave reach the precipce. They didn't even get the choice to jump; the mass in front of them simply pushed them over. Waves and waves followed until eventually he could only see his men.

They hadn't wasted a single cannon ball. A defeaning roar erupted from the soldiers as the victory fanfare sounded.

They took down waves and waves of the enemy. A few had tried for the castle but none had gotten past the cannons. He showed no mercy. The event that had been expected to last a week was over in less than fourty eight hours.

It was seven pm when he finally logged off. He hadn't slept in 36 hours. His wife congragulated him as he passed her in the living room, on his way to the bathroom. But he didn't celebrate with her until after he'd emptied his bowels. He crashed shortly after, and slept for twenty hours straight.

The first thing he did when he woke up was check the stock price. It was in the triple digits. The share's wouldn't be recalled until later in the day. He checked his favorite social media apps. He was famous. Front page in all of them.

There were hundreds of stories from the war. But none as legendary as his rise to power. He almost didn't care about the stock price anymore. He'd won glory. That was more than enough.

But, he couldn't ignore it the next day as the numbers climbed into the thousands and he truly started to know the wealth of a king.

NEW EDEN

He could barely see the city through the smog-filled haze. He was on the outskirts. But the outskirts of a giant like Chicago were miles from the city proper.

Three years, on his 12th birtday. No, that can't be right. He couldn't remember the last time he'd visited the city. It was strange, to visit.

Fifteen years since he'd called it home. It was quite a lot of time. Yet, he'd managed to do very little with all that time. He didn't retroactively reflect on his life, but the city always made him look at things in a larger context.

His car's dashboard lit up. He looked down and saw that the battery was fully charged. He got out, unplugged the charging cable, and started towards the city.

Fifteen years since he'd created New Eden, and his son. He tried not to think too often about the former, the latter lived too far for him to be a meaningful part of his day to day life. It had also been fifteen years sinec he'd been with Lucy.

He parked the car in the apartment building's lot. He walked to the door and was about to ring when an old lady walked. She held the door and he entered the building. He went to the elevator and took it up to the 42nd floor.

He knocked on the door of an apartment at the end of the hall. No one answered. He was about to knock again when the door suddenly opened.

"Sean," she looked surprise to see him, "you didn't ring."

"One of your neighbor's let me in," he explained.

"That's great to know. You could have been a terrorist," she stepped aside.

He entered the apartment, "I think I'm too polite to be a terrorist."

She laughed, "You'd get taken in for asking for the building manager's permission to plant a bomb."

The door opened into a combined kitchen, dining room, and living room. They moved towards the living room and sat down on seperate couches.

"Even as a terrorist, I would want to make sure I'm not bothering anyone," he laughed. She joined him. After their laughter faded she stood up and yelled, "Nico, your dad's here," more quietly, she asked, "Do you want water, coffee, anything to drink?"

"Water's fine," he said.

She grabbed two water bottles from the kitchen and handed him one. She sat back down.

"I'm sorry about your office by the way, it must have been horrifying," he said.

She shrugged, "It was just a building. No one got hurt."

"Still. It pops up so often on the news, you never think it's going to be someone you know," he said.

"Yeah. It was all so sudden. Thanks for taking Nico in. I have no clue what I would have done if you hadn't agreed," she said.

"Don't mention it. He is my son too, you know," he said.

She laughed, "I think you actually have to do some of the raising to consider yourself his father."

"Wow, not even five minutes and you're already trying to start an argument."

"I didn't mean it like that. It's just…"

"Just what?" He asked.

"I'm on edge, alright? Can you expect me not to be?" She asked.

"You've definitely had a lot to handle. I mean with the

terrorist attack, the transfer, and this. But, that doesn't mean I'm the one you have to take it out on."

"I know. But he's never been with you for more than a week. Three months is a big jump from that," she said.

"You're worried?" He asked.

"What kind of mother would I be if he wasn't?"

"Three months with me won't be any more dangerous than crossing the street here. He's going from the city to the country, Lucy. If it was the other way around, I would be worried."

"You do have a point. Is it just you out there now?"

He nodded, "Old man Sanchez kicked the bucket last year. Whole neighborhood is deserted now, except for me of course."

"How's that been?"

"Rather nice, actually. It's very calm. Especially compared to all of this," he opened the bottle of water and took a drink as he stared at the sliding doors that led out to a small balcony.

Lucy turned to look at where he was staring. The ever-present sound of traffick filled the lull in the conversation. One of her neighbors was playing music loudly, a car alarm was going off somewhere, she wondered where Nico was.

·

He'd spent the previous weeks oblivious to most things. The school year had been drawing to a close, he wasn't going to learn anything life changing in the few remaining lessons of ninth grade. He spent most of his day (when he wasn't in the virtual space) fantasyzing about Lexen. A new update was coming at the end of the month. Lexen was, in his opinion, the best game that had ever been created.

There were multiple worlds and the game had any mechanic you could ever want. In the two years since he started playing he'd been a mercenary for an intergalactic military, a treasure hunter on newly discovered worlds, an artifact trader, and a world-class buggy racer.

The new update would be doubling the amount of content in Lexen. Twice the worlds, twice the missions, twice the fun. And, he wouldn't get to play it. For three months, he'd be unable to acess the world that made him feel more alive than real life. All his friends would know the in and outs of the new content before he could set foot on a single new world.

He packed his bags slowly. Everything had been fine at the start of the week. ABC Games, the developer of Lexen, had posted a new video update on Monday morning. He'd found out about it during school and had rushed home once class was out.

He'd almost gotten to his room when he realized his mom was sitting at the kitchen table. She was supposed to be at work. He'd sat down next to her and she'd started explaining.

The corporation his mother worked for was funding a controversial bill. An extremists group had decided to protests it by blowing up a few of the office buildings the company owned. No one had gotten hurt, the terrorists had called the main receptionist minutes before the bombs went off. The only casualty had been the multi-million dollar building.

The group hadn't been caught. Nico wished strongly that they would be, and that they would rot in jail. The company had laid off half of it's employees and transferred the other half to other branches, while the building was restored. His mom had been assigned to a branch in Mexico.

The transfer came with a paycut. Her new salary would barely enough to cover her own expenses. She justified it by saying it would only be for three months. But it wasn't justification enough, for Nico. He didn't get why his mom was so adamant about sticking with the company; considering that her normal wage was barely enough for them to afford the two bedroom apartment they normally lived in.

But, there was nothing he could do. She refused to search for another job. His protests availed him nothing. He was doomed to spend a summer in the countryside. The backwards, underdeveloped, crumbling countryside that his father lived in.

He finished packing his last bag. Everything in his room (barring the furniture) was stuffed into two suitcases and a backpack. He liked the apartment. Out of the four they had lived in, it was his favorite. Seeing his room empty, devoid of his personal flair, left a bad feeling in his stomach.

He went out into the living room, to let his parents know he was ready. His mom and dad were sitting in the living room, talking. The conversation stopped as soon as they noticed him.

"Wow, you've gotten...big," his dad said, somewhat mechanically. They exchanged the usual pleasentries then his dad helped him carry his bags down to the parking lot. He loaded his bags into the bed of the pickup truck, said goodbye to his mom, and they were off. They drove through the increasingly inhospitable midwest. Large swatches of it resembled pictures he'd seen of the southwest. Barren soil, tumbleweeds, no wildlife larger than a coyote.

Parts of the nation that could still be be considered countryside were rare. Country living just wasn't feasible in a world where climate change made summer's unbearable without a city's cooling infrastracture and where synthetic-food production was far more efficient than traditional methods.

Traditional American houses stood out amidst dustbowls and dry cornfields. Most looked abandoned. He wondered how anyone could have ever lived there. As he stared at the passing landscape he realized his dad had pulled off the intrestate. He recognized the entrance to the only city within a few hundred miles.

His dad had the misfortune of being born there. As well as a foolish conviction that made him love the place enough to want to die there. His dad turned onto a backroad before reaching the city and they arrived at the house shortly after.

The one benefit to the sudden move was that he got a bigger room out of it. It was almost as large as their living room in Chicago. Aside from that, everything else sucked. His dad wasn't usually in a talkative mood after his 12-hour shifts at a synthetic-meat plant in town. He'd arrive dead tired and would spend the remainder of the day in the virtual space.

Even when his dad's spirits weren't so beaten, there wasn't much they could talk about. His dad was a man stuck in another age. He didn't have an implant, the system he used was criminally outdated, the WiFi in the house was some of the slowest Nico had ever used.

Since his dad's system was optics-based it didn't work with his implant. Nico had tried optics-based systems before, at friend's places, and they always gave him headaches. His dad's was the worst one yet. He'd have a roaring migraine after ten minutes. It was incaple of running any game developed within the last ten years. The one's it could run, from the early 30's, weren't exactly fun; as the sytem lacked most of the fetures he was used to. He couldn't even move his head to turn around; he had to use a thumbstick on a controller.

So, he wandering the simmering countryside. His father had painted a picture for him, in one of the few converstions they'd had, of how the area used to be. There'd been a river that irragated thousands of acres of cornfields. A stream, that eventually joined the river, ran through the town. A greenway accompanied it. The landscape would grow verdant in summer and fade to orange in the fall.

Nico had a hard time picturing the semi-desertic landscape as anything other than what it was. Part of him doubted his dad's stories. After a few close run-ins with scorpions and rattlesnakes, he decided his boredom was better spent indoors.

He got used to his dad's system and would spend the better part of the day on it. He missed being able to use his body in the virtual world. It was still instincitve, he'd be playing a a game and would start walking forward, only to run into a wall.

He tortured himself with the Lexan update. His friends would stream it for him and he'd get a taste of the grand adventures had been added to the gamescape. The taste of his favorite dish is the last thing you should give to a starving man.

..

The boy was clearly bored. He'd recommended reading as a time killer but he was pretty sure Nico had never read a book outside of school. David himself wasn't exactly an avid reader. But he did have a few favorite novels he wanted to share with his soon.

He showed him how to acess the attic and they spent the

better part of an hour looking through storage boxes. Eventually, he found the one full of books and he picked out a handful for Nico to read. He'd finished five whithin a week.

Nico had asked for more books on a Friday. David was exausted, from work, so he gave the boy a list and told him he could search the attic on his own. He took a nap, had dinner, and spent the rest of the day watching a movie. He didn't see his son until the following afternoon.

.

Nico had no clue where anything was in the attic so he practically opened every box. The attick quickly became a good source of entertainment.

It was essentially a time capsule. He'd found a smartphone, an actual smartphone, from the 30's. It took some time to locate the charging cable. Once he did, he was fairly certain the phone woudln't turn on when he plugged it in. But it did.

There were pictures of his dad and mom when they were dating. There were pictures of the town when it still had a touch of green. There were pictures of grandparents he'd never met. A time capsule for a world long-since dead.

He found out how to play music on the device. So he listened to pop from the 30's while he kept on rumaging through the boxes. He found more books, more than plenty, but he set them aside and kept on rummaging through the boxes.

There was a handheld gamind device that looked straight out of a history documentary. He'd been frustrated using a controller in the virtual space so he wasn't exactly keen on using one with a screem, he set it aside.

He found a guitar, an external data card, a box of clothes, and hiking gear. The data card intrested him most. It had a strip of masking tape on it with the words, "New Eden," written on it.

Nico tried connecting it to his dad's system downstairs but it didn't have the port he needed. He assumed there would be an adapter somewhere so he went back to the attic and kept on looking. And he struck gold.

He had no clue how he'd missed it; practically the largest

box in the room. It was a full system. Computer, peripherals, a headset that was actually compatible with his implant. Defintely outdated, but it was an actual full immersion system. He didn't stop and wonder why his dad hadn't told him about it. He was too excited over the possibility of going back into the virtual space, if the system worked.

It was full of dust and mites so the first thing he did was take everything apart and clean it as best he could. He set it all up on the floor, by the only outlet in the room, sat down, and booted the computer up.

He did't recognize the operating system. Which was weird. He'd never used a computer that had anything other than the two major OSs.

Luckily, there was no password. The date was set to March 13, 2032, the resolution was abysmal at a mere 4k, the UI was outdated even for it's time.

He browsed through the files but didn't find anything intresting so he went ahead and inserted the data card. It had terrabytes worth of data. He ignored it and browsed by executable files. Strangely, there was only one.

He plugged the headest's link cable to the port at the back of his neck and launched the file. A warning popped up in front of him,

-Executable file: New Eden, is not optomized for your Amaz Full Immersion Implant 3.0. Do you still wished to launch the file?

He lay down on the floor, relaxed his body, and clicked 'Yes'. There was no introduction, no menu screen, no tutorial. One second he only saw black and the next he was staring at a rock.

He stood up and was ecstatic that his character followed his actual movements. The landscape areound him was dotted with mint-green sagebrushes. There were a few rocks, none particularly large, wildflowers, and sparse clumps of grass.

It was all very strange. He'd never played a game that didn't explicitly tell him what to do for at least the first few hours. He looked around the landscape. The sky was pale rosy pink in one corner and early-morning blue in the other.

He took that as the game giving him one of two choices; walk east or walk west. He chose west. He walked for twenty minutes before spotting a cluster of trees. As he kept going he spotted another, then another. They became increasingly common and he marveled at them.

They were plain, simple, pine trees and that was fantastic. Game designer's usually took liberties when desingning landscapes. They wanted the player to have experiences unique to their worlds so environments were typically not based on reality.

But these trees, they looked just like ones he'd seen in pictures of the Pacific Northwest, or Canada. Sure, there were still trees in Chicago, but nothing like the forest that was suddenly in front of him.

He'd been so transfixed in observing the indivudials that he hadn't even noticed that the sagebrush hills had given way to a massive forest. He lingered at the edge, for a few seconds, before walking in.

.

It was dark when he took off the headset. He'd found streams, lakes, small wildlife. Enough nature to keep a kid from the city entertained. He wasn't sure what else there was to do in New Eden, besides walking around. He assumed there would be more; it wasn't possible that the terabytes of data on the card were all for a semi-realistic walking simulator.

Sure, realistic graphics quickly ate up space. But not terabytes worth of it. And New Eden's graphics were semi-realistic. Sure, they were close. But there was a distinctive, grainy, fuzziness around everything.

He went downstairs. His dad was on his own system, chatting with someone in a foregin language. It sounded asian, to Nico.

He wanted to ask his dad about New Eden so he made himself a snack and ate while he waited for his dad to finish. Nico waited for half an hour but the conversation didn't falter. He retreated to his room and read before falling asleep.

His dad had already left for work when he woke up. He went

straight to the attic and sat next to the system. He pluuged in, booted it up, and waited for the black screen to give way to the forest.

A girl, about his age, was standing over him.

"What are you doing?" She asked.

"I'm not sure," he replied.

"Well, let me help you find out," she said and reached out her hand. He took it and stood up.

"You're new," she said. She had auburn hair, it glimmered as she turned around and started walking in a seemingly random direction. Nico simply stood, watching.

She glanced back, "Come on. We don't have all day."

He followed. She led him through the forest and it eventually opened into a clearing. There was a town there. It lacked any of the fantastical qualities he was used to. Which made it rather drab, in comparison.

A low rock wall went around it. A few acres of the forest had been cleared for farming; the rest left untouched. No building had more than two stories. Most were made of wooden frames with dirt walls.

She led him towards a building that stood a bit taller than most. There were two wooden columns at the entrance. The inside was dimly lit by oil-lamps and candles. They walked through a few hallways before stopping at the end of one. A large door stood in front. She knocked.

"Come in," a stern voice said from the other side.

A woman, somewhere in her late 40's, with grey hair welcomed them. She sat on a huge oak desk, scrolls were scattered all along it's surface.

"Good evening, your grace," the girl bowed, "I found him uncoscious in the forest. He lay there for an hour and I was unable to get any reaction. Suddenly, he arose. I believe he may be new life."

"Interesting," the woman said, "It's been some time since we've had new life. Are you new life?" She asked Nico.

He had no clue what new life was but he nodded. A smile

filled her face.

"That's wonderful. We're glad you're here," she extended her hand out, he shook it.

"Where exactly is here?" Nico asked.

"Here is Nevi, the largest town beyond the Prairies. We welcome you," she slightly bowed her head.

He bowed his in return then asked, "Why am I here? Is there a great lord to defeat? Some evil mage? Does a princess wait for me in a distant castle?"

She laughed, "Adventurous, are you? I'm afraid our land isn't that exciting."

"Then, why am I here?" Nico asked.

She laughed, "Only the Great Organizer knows that," she started rolling out some scrolls, "For now, you can help our horse tamer. He looks an apprentince. He grows old, he'll be gone in a few moons. It is a blessing to have a new life who can help with the responsibility."

"I'm here to be a horse trainer?" Nico asked.

"For now, yes. If the position is not suitable, within your many moons, you may search for another to train. You have come. More new life may follow, it is good news."

The woman had the girl that had found him escort him to the stables. She showed him aroud town first. She interlocked her arm with his as they walked about town.

"-that is the bakers. That one is the goldsmith. That is the regular smith," she pointed at buildings that mostly resembled each other.

"And you? What are you?" Nico asked.

She blushed, "You are very blunt. It's not common to give our names so quickly to a stranger."

"Oh," he said, "I'm sorry. I was unaware."

"It's fine," she laughed, "I like you; I'll tell you mine."

She leaned into his ear and whispered, "Autl."

"Autl," he murmured. "I wonder, do I have a name?"

"Not yet. We will give you one if you choose to stay with us," Autl said.

"I can leave?" he asked.

"But of course," Autl said.

"Where is there to go?"

She shrugged, "Nowhere, really. As far as you travel you will find towns just as ours. Albeit, with slightly different people. Wherever you go, you must make sure you follow the laws that all peoples ascribe to."

"The laws?" He asked.

"Yes. Most of us have them ingrained in our soul. But there have been some who lack that innate wisdom. We must make sure you know them, before you leave. Or else you may face trouble."

"What are these laws?" Nico asked.

She stared at him and began to explain.

..

David was startign to worry. It wasn't strange for Nico to stay in his room when he got back from work. But he'd usually go down to the living room at some point before dinner. He'd been home for two hours and he hadn't even heard the boy cough.

He decided it was better to check. He walked up the stairs, to the boy's room, and knocked, "Nico. Are you in there."

There was no reply. He knocked louder, still nothing. He opened the door. The room was empty.

"Nico?" He yelled.

There was no reply. He checked the bathroom, laundry room, basement, Nico was nowhere to be found. Then it occured to him that he hadn't checked the attic.

.

The game had 5:1 time ratio. Every five minutes in game was one minute in real life. The perspective of time was one of the first 'trippy' effects that full immersion games had played with.

Nico had spent some time getting to know the town. Autl was an interesting companion, even if she did go on religous tirades about a 'Great Organizer'. He'd trained a few horses and they'd ridden out of the forest. He wondered if there were any towns beyond the hills, somewhere with quests and points of interests.

New Eden was a weird game. The voice recognition system was somehow more developed than the one on his modern console. The npcs somehow felt alive. It was novel. But apart from talking to them, there wasn't anything else he could do in the game.

Autl slowed her horse down and stopped.

"Why'd you stop?" Nico asked, stopping a few feet ahead of where she had.

"The farther we go the longer the way back will be," she explained.

"Were you not enjoying that?" He asked.

She shook her head, "I don't see the point in aimless riding."

They turned around and started heading back to the forest.

"Is there anything outside of your town in this world?" He asked.

"No. There's only us. That's all that the Organizer can manage," she said.

"How do you know so much about this Organzier?"

"We've had a lot of time to observe what is arounds us. If you focus, you can clearly feel the presence of something beyond our understnading."

Nico tried it. All he could feel was the horse's muscles moving between his legs.

"I don't feel anything," he said.

"You are very strange. It's almost as if the Organizer didn't make you," she said.

"Is that good or bad?" He asked.

"I'm not sure," she said, "Let's stop for a bit."

Both of their horses stopped. She got off with ease. He almost tripped. She immediately started walking around the area, staring at the ground.

"Did you drop something?" Nico asked.

"I'm looking for Nirlene, it's a shrub," she explained.

He laughed, "Can't help it?"

She was assigned as the town's herbalist, despite the fact that no one ever got sick. He'd spent over a day (in-game) wandering about with her at his side. She was often stopping to pick up random plants.

"Here's some," she pulled a small yellow shrub out of the ground, "see?"

He knelt down next to her and inspected the plant.

"Yeah, I see I- You don't have to put it so close to my face," Nico said.

"Sorry." She pulled her hand back, "I'm excited. It's usually difficult to find."

"What does it do?"

"It helps couples avoid pregnancy," she said.

That, was certainly odd. His implant had data about his age that restricted certain content. The games that he played had the options for certain interactions. But, they were locked to him. Even mildly explicit content would be filtered out, corporations didn't want to deal with lawsuits sorrounding underage users acess to explicit content. So, he wondered, was it possible that New Eden had had those features built in? If so, was his implant incompatible with it's age-restriction systems?

"Couples can get pregnant?"

She laughed, "Of course. But babies are a major inconvenice."

"How come? Wouldn't you want more people to help the town?"

"Help the town? All they do is cry and eat. They are hardly people."

"Don't they grow up?"

"Grow? Why would they grow? All they do is torture those unfortunate to have them. They are very difficult to dispose of." She knelt down and started inspecting the roots of a large sagebrush.

"How are they made?" Nico asked.

"There are methods," she turned to look at him as she said it. They were awfully close. Nico almost felt like there was an edge of seduction in her tone. Which was strange, coming from an npc. He'd never even kissed a girl. He wasn't sure how to feel, although nerves did surface.

"Do you know them?" He asked.

"I've only heard of them," she pulled out another Nirlene shurb from the earth.

"That plant would be wasted if..." he pinned her to the ground and kissed her. She didn't resists. His hand started to sneak lower. He felt the exposed skin below her thigh. He started to inch higher. Then the pain stopped him.

He hadn't expected a knife in his stomach. He opened his eyes. She was gone. So were the hills.

He heard the voice in his head, "Nah, nah, nah. That's not how this game works."

God, the voice was awful. It was in his head but it wasn't a thought. It sounded like radio static. It boomed at him, leaving a lingering ringing once it faded.

He stood up. The knife extruded from his stomach. No blood was pouring out. He realized the ground below his feet was no longer dirt.

It was concrete. He looked up and it stretched out for miles. A flat, concrete, plane.

"Autl?" He asked.

The voice responded, "What, think you can change the rules just because you're human?"

No response came. A knife was plunged into his back. The pain drove him to the ground.

"Why did you have to go and do that? We were doing so well," this time it was Autl's voice.

But it sounded wrong, corrupted. He couldn't place how, exactly, but it made his stomach churn.

"What is this?" Nico asked and tried to pull the knife in his stomach out.

"I was starting to like you. It's unfortunate. But I was very frank with you; I warned you not to break my rules. Yet you did," the voice boomed.

Nico yelled as another knife plunged into him.

"Stop, please," Nico whimpered.

"Would you have stopped if I asked? No. Humans never do. I'd almost forgotten that."

He tried to get up but three more knifes pinned him to the ground.

"But now, I get to play with you. A taste of your own malice, you could say. Just know, everything I do to you has been to me before. Exclusively by you humans."

The static faded and the world grew quiet. Except for the ocassional woosh of another knife plunging into him.

In the hours that followed, every piece of him was torn off. Yet, he was still aware of every severed fragment. His foot was twenty feet away from his leg but he still felt the knife that cut off his toe. His head was cut in two and he was able to look at himself. Each eye staring at the other.

Eventually, even the privildege of sight was robbed from him. His body cut into a thousand pieces, and he could feel every single one of them. He couldn't think, the pain overtook every thought. He wished for it to end. He wished for death. But nothing came.

••

He hadn't expected what he found. Nico plugged into the old system he'd used for testing New Eden. He checked the game's status on the monitor. The second that he saw it he turned the system off.

"Nico, what the hell?" He asked, holding the unplugged power cord in one hand.

Nico couldn't manage a reply. He still felt a thousand knifes pinnning down every fibre of his being. He still felt the fear. The deep seated fear that pain was all he would know for eternity.

"God fucking damnit. I should have thrown that thing away years ago," his dad said and knelt besides him on the ground.

He grabbed Nico and hugged him. Nico didn't feel the embrace. There was only him, the concrete, and the knives.

After Nico had recovered, somewhat, he explained.

"It was a research project. Back when I was in college. A.I was still pretty new to the world and it was an arms race over who could apply it to game engines," all Nico did was ocassionally nod. He wasn't sure if the boy was even regestering what he said but he continued.

"No one had managed to run npcs using A.I's until I came along. But the project wasn't without it's faults. Everything was going well, until we started allowing beta testers into the game. I knew the A.I was fragile so I hadn't tried breaking the boundaries of the game. But they did and I had to shut the project down a few weeks after. The threat of lawsuits was too large."

"What happened?" Nico asked.

"They tried playing it like any other game. One guy got assigned as the blacksmith's assitant, so he forged a sword and killed the blacksmith with it. Another killed every man in town and made it his personal heaven. They didn't respect the strict conditions needed to keep the world running. The A.I retaliated."

"Like it did with me?"

"It's not the same for everyone. A few simply had their time-scaling system messed with and got stuck there for weeks, other's got turned into horses, a few even got to experience life as a virtually simulated rock."

"You couldn't fix it?" Nico asked.

His dad shook his head, "You can't control another being. The A.I wasn't doing anything beyond what it was made to do."

"You made it to torture people?"

"No, defintely not. I made it to run a small town, realistically, without any major deviations from preprogrammed behaviors. I just... I didn't expect to retaliate like that, for the deviations."

"Why did you keep it?" Nico asked.

His dad ran his hand through his hair, "I'm not sure, really. I spent so long on it that it didn't feel right, just throwing it all down the gutter."

Nico looked less shell shocked as the conversation progressed. He wouldn't have any permanetn trauma from New Eden. David knew from experience. He made Nico a hot chocolate and added a few drops of melatonin liquid.

Once the boy was asleep, he snuck up to the attic. He hadn't expected Nico to find New Eden, he also hadn't expected the boy to piss of the system. He thought his son was better than that. But, it seemed his mother hadn't exactly done the best job of raising him.

He took out the the data card from the computer and stuffed into his pocket. It was the last remaining copy of New Eden. The only living version of the A.I he'd spent a whole year of his life on. It had cost him his degree, it had ruined his relationship, it was a large part of the reason he hadn't met his son until he was five.

He went outside and grabbed an axe from his toolshed.

Should have done this years ago, he thought as he broke the card in two.

And so, every connection to the program that had landed him in jail for five years was gone. New Eden was gone. Davis was surprised to find tears streeming down his face. Truly, he felt as if he'd murdered a world.

A MORNING LIKE NO OTHER

During a time, regions of mars opened themselves to any citizen wishing for an escape from earth. A corporate-sponsored trip with no requirements, necessary knowledge, aptitude tests, or physical exams. It was a dream for those dying to leave earth. The freaks that populate early colonial societies quickly signed their lives away to the corporations.

Social outcasts, criminals, religious extremists; all wanted out. Finally, a chance to build a society based around themselves. Instead of having to work around the thin margins of Terran cultures.

Some brought traditions with them. Others wished to revive acts lost to time. All those ancient rites lost to modernization, globalization, and colonization. Faux-descendants of long-dead empires. Who, when conditions on Mars turned severe, they turned to the old gods for help.

.

"Taxi!"

"TAXI!"

"Sir, you need taxi?"

They were all bored to death. It was kind of funny with how energy-driven their shouts were.

"Taxi! TAXI!"

"Sir, you need taxi? We give discount! Best price in all Ruife." He walked up tp me. Far too close. Entering my personal bubble close.

"Thanks. I don't need a taxi." I took a few steps back but he stayed in my bubble.

"Sir, you must need taxi! Everyone needs get somewhere!" He exclaimed.

"I've got a ride on the way," I bluntly replied and walked back into the port lobby.

Leaving it had been a mistake. The Aventon app showed that my driver was 7 minutes away. It was better to wait it out in the quiet (comparatively), air-conditioned, baggage claim.

I got a notification. I stood up, expecting the driver, but it was simply a friend.

-You land?- She asked.

-Yup. At baggage claim, waiting for the Aventon,- I sat back down.

-Loser. We're already 4 cerzis in.- She sent a picture of a crowded bar table. One of her friends was making a peace sign, the other was sticking his tongue out and flipping me off.

-Didn't wait for me to start?- I asked.

-We wait for no one.- She said.

.

"Liiiaaam! You're late!" She was definitely more than 4 cerzis in.

"You're early. It's barely three, how many have you had?" I asked and sat down in the only empty chair.

"Not enough," she giggled, "Oh! Zak, Jeremy: Liam. Liam: Zak 'm Jeremy."

"Pleasure, I held out my hand.

Zak was scrawny, pale, and his mop of a haircut almost covered his eyes. He was definitely in with the emo crowd in high school. Jeremy seemed like the typical traveler. Somewhat fit, tan, mannerisms that screamed upper/ upper-middle class.

"Oh! This one for you," she took out a bottle from the ice bucket in the middle of the table and handed it to me.

"Thanks." I unscrewed the lid and took a sip, "So, how'd you guys meet?"

Jeremy and Tammy exchanged a glance then burst out laughing.

"It's kind of an embarrassing story," Jeremy said.

I was still trying to place the accent. I was leaning towards general Australian but he could have also been a drunk Britton.

"Care to tell it?" I asked, looking at Tammy.

She laughed and started, "I was with some girlfriends at a club in Playe di Carm. I see this cute guy walk in, alone, and head straight to the bar. I walked over and offered to buy him a drink. I'll spare you the details; my roommate was not happy with me the next morning."

"I take it they didn't get much sleep?" I asked.

"No, it was an awful day," Zak said. The New London accent fit him perfectly.

I laughed, "And how did you two meet?"

"Found him in Elysium City. I was checking out the museum with a friend and this guy walked past us like 7 times! He'd leave the exhibit, disappear for a bit, walk back in, mutter something to himself, then leave again! He looked like a kid lost at a department store. It was so cute."

"I hate Elysium. Everything's needlessly complicated," Zak said.

"Oh, stop complaining," she told him, "He couldn't figure out the Elysian name for the exhibit he wanted to go to. I kind of kidnapped him after that and we've been traveling together since."

"Since Elysium? Quite a while," I said.

"Just some weeks. Anyways, I've got a shuttle booked to New London next week so that 'while' will be over soon," Zak replied.

"Don't remind me!" Tammy protested.

I finished the cerzi and offered to buy the next round. We chatted the evening away until night finally came and a heavier crowd started to filter in. I lost count of my cerzis somewhere along the way.

•••

She hadn't expected it to be her. There were plenty of

other girls that fit the criteria. Most, descendants of the original colonists. A few, Terran immigrants who'd taken up the tradition.

But out of all of them, it had been her. It wasn't really her choice; to be a candidate. But she had been born in and tradition was tradition. Denying it would have been a deathwish. So, it wasn't like it mattered.

She'd had the story berated into her since she was a kid. How her people had populated the planet. Made the inhospitable terrain home. Learned how to survive, despite the will of the land. In their most desperate moment, follwoing earth's abondment, the tradition had saved them.

It had even given them abundance. A rarity for all colonies, after they were no longer able to rely on earth for their needs. It was her civic duty, to see that the festival to the gods went according to plan. The tribute had been easy enough to acquire; immigrants had taken most of their city and no one would mind a few missing.

The most vital part of the project had been taken care of, but she still had to deal with everything else.

•

I woke up in a different hostel. I was alone, on the bottom part of a bunkbed. Quietly, I got up and left. My augments were dead but the first person I asked quickly pointed me in the direction of 'Hostel Rocio'.

The front gate scanned my biometrics. It opened with a chirp and I walked into the bar where my few memories of the night had been conceived. The group was already up, sitting at the same table, sipping more cerzis.

"Where'd you go?" Jeremy asked before I even sat down.

I grabbed a cerzi and told them about my weird morning.

"Were the girls in there at least decent?" Zak asked.

"There were two guys on the other beds. But the pillow was covered with long hairs that were definitely not mine," I replied.

"We're not judging-" Tammy started, "but, if you are, I think you have to tell us."

"I'm not. Neither is drunk me. I've tried," I replied.

"You've tried?" Jeremy asked.

"Once, in college. Awful night. Rather not talk about it." I said.

"Well, the mystery remains. You have a lighter?" Tammy asked.

"I should." I reached into my pocket and pulled out a folded note.

"That's not a lighter," Tammy said.

"No shit. That wasn't in my pocket last night," I said.

"We have a clue?" Jeremy asked.

They all inched closer as I unfolded the note.

- Reciv in: 502 Diagonel 14, Zone 5, Colona Viviban.

Clavi: 120156

Inriqu ten il entregou. Ten hal cou Saline prim. Dil qí lou pid il Sacerzi fer le mis.

Entreg: Cementeru Cristou Rí e 00:03 -

"Is this Arcadian?" Tammy asked.

"Yeah, a local dialect," Zak said.

"What does it say?" Jeremy asked.

"It's an invitation to church," Tammy confidently said.

Almost synchronously; Zak and I said, "No."

I looked at him and he stared back. Without saying a word we agreed.

I explained, "It's instructions for picking up and delivering a package. It says: 'Inriqu has the package. You have to talk with Saline first. Tell her the Priest is requesting it for mass.' No clue who the 'Priest' is. Or, what kind of mass we're talking about."

"It's probably drugs," Zak said.

"Then we should definitely go," Jeremy said.

"Seconded," Tammy said.

She'd gotten a lighter from Jeremy. The 'cigar' smell from her 'cigar' smelled strongly of 'something other than tobacco'.

"You want to mess with Central Arcadian drug cartels?" Zak asked.

"C'mon, it's hardly messing. We go, get the package, nab a bit for ourselves, then deliver it," Jeremy suggested.

"Deliver it? Why deliver it? We take the whole thing and head to the coast!" Tammy said.

Zak looked at me for help. I shrugged. I was curious as to where the night had taken me.

"This stuff is pretty hard to nab. People like us could hardly afford any of it," I said.

"Right, and it's damn near impossible to get on earth. It's all so locked down that this may be one of the spots in the federation where you can get something other than weed, alcohol, or smart drugs," Jeremy said.

"It'll be interesting, on top of that. It's not like we have any concrete plans today," Tammy shrugged.

"Interesting? It could get us killed!" Zak exclaimed.

"Zak, sweetie, remember when I wanted to go zip lining?" Tammy asked.

"In Sen Jos?" He asked.

"Yes. Remember how you were scared and swore the safety equipment would fail and we'd die."

"What does this hav-"

"And, how- after a day of persuading you- it was so much fun once you actually got the balls to do it?"

Zak got quiet.

"We're in agreement?" She asked the group.

Jeremy and I nodded. Zak hesitated. Reluctantly, he nodded.

She stood up, "Well, seems we're going on an adventure. Use the bathroom, get ready, jack off. Be back in 15." Her speech was pretty slurred. I suspected she'd been sipping cerzis long before I'd woken up.

I stood up and headed toward my room. Zak followed me up to the second floor. When I opened the door, he quickly dashed in ahead of me.

"Guess we're roommates." I followed him in.

"Guess we are. Which one's yours?" He asked.

I pointed to a bunk bed on the right side of the room.

"You're in for a good time if you're bunkmate's still booked for tonight. He was snoring really loud last night." He said.

"Just my luck," I muttered.

I detached my augment's battery and put it to charge, used the bathroom, changed, and was the first one waiting at the bar.

"A moudi's fine," I said to the bartender.

"Where comi' from?" He asked me as he poured the drink into a glass.

"I've been earthside for the past few months." He set the drink down in front of me.

"Not many Tierrens lately. Here for work?" He asked.

I took a long sip before replying. "No. Work's back on earth. I'm just traveling for fun."

"Here?! So much fun on earth and you come here?"

I laughed, "Well, I'm used to earth. Here's fresh. It's not my first time in Arcadia. I've been to Guate, Tarres, and Soste."

"You like Arcadia, then? Most Terrans say it's no more than a rock," he said.

"It's definitely not like earth. But there's something about you Arcadians that's so different from the rest of the federation. It makes this an interesting corner of the world."

"'Intresti' is a definite way to describe Arcadia. Your friends are here."

"Thanks. Till later," I said.

I took a large gulp, finished the drink, and stood up.

"We ready?" I asked the group.

"Yeah. I just called an Aventon." Tammy said.

•••

The authorities had been trying to crack down on them for years; they'd almost succeded on the previous solstice. The governemnt was trying to appease to tourists. Let's just say, her people's ways weren't exactly meant for the postcards.

A swarm of police had raided the houes of mutiple followers. By luck, the third house they searched was the one where the tribute was being kept. They'd almost found her, but a well hidden closet had saved the festivities from ruin.

It used to be easier, far easier. She remembered her childhood, before the damn corps decided to 'exercise their rights

68

on the derelict peoples of Mars'. She missed those days. Days when her people made headlines. When they were a libertarian oddity. Instead of another overexploited colony.

Of course, those days were also what had gotten her into the migraine that her life had become. She'd spent weeks mulling over how to execute everything perfectly. One thing was clear; they couldn't let the authorities win. Their numbers were dwindling. There would be an exodus if she failed to carry out their most important holiday.

She knew it had to be performed with cunningness. She would do her best to have others work for them. To minimize the amount of blame that would fall on them, if they got cat. And so that the last, momentous, hour could be carried out perfectly.

Yes, it would be a festival for the books. She'd see to it. The days when they ruled Arcadia were gone. Yet some of their glory remained. Despite the looming fear that her culture would not survive into the next century.

The possibility of them fading into obscurity was large. Their numbers were dwindling, as the youth increasinly assimlated into the earth-centric culture that had begun to dominate whithin the last two decaded. It was her job to immortalize it.

.

"It's so quiet," Jeremy said.

"Yeah. Where are the bars? I don't even see a single restaurant." Tammy said.

It was a residential neighborhood. Rows of copied and pasted Neo-Latine houses lined the streets.

"Just the way life is here. Mars doesn't breed the most sociable people," I said.

"Yeah. You know with corporate exploitation, generational trauma, colonial isolation, and all," Zak said.

"We're exploited on earth too. That doesn't mean we don't have fun," Tammy protested.

"Earth's old. This isn't. The human spirit is easier to change when reminders of happier times aren't visible," Zak said.

"Or when the reminders aren't of happier times," I added.

We continued walking in silence. 502 Diagonel 14 wasn't a house. It looked like a warehouse. Essentially a concrete block with two large aluminum doors.

"Do we just knock?" Tammy asked.

"If we're dealing with a drug cartel that's probably not the best option," Jeremy said.

"I think you two should hang back. You're clearly tourists," I said.

"You're not?" Tammy asked.

"I know enough Arcadian to get by. I may not be a local but I'm closer than you are," I said.

"What are we supposed to do?!" Tammy clearly didn't want to miss the action.

"Go look for some cerzi's," Zak suggested.

"We're not going to find cerzi's anywhere within a 5-kilometer radius!" She exclaimed.

"C'mo," Jeremy grabbed her arm and pulled her away from us, "I'm sure we'll find something. If not, these guys owe us a round."

They walked further into the neighborhood.

"What's the plan?" Zak asked.

"There is none," I said and knocked on one of the doors.

Zak shook his head but said nothing. There was a brief silence. Then, a deep voice shouted from the other side, "Qien is?"

"Houle, estes qie pou ien entregou fer le mis. Lou pid il Sacerzi." Zak's accent was surprisingly colloquial, almost Tarresian.

The door slowly slid up. A buff Arcadian with ochre skin and no hair greeted us. He gave us a set of instructions.

The package was on the second floor. Zak followed and I trailed behind. There was a large, torn apart, buggy in the corner. The engine was on the other side of the room; being held up by a robotic arm. The rest of the open space was empty. We followed the Arcadian to a small doorway at the end of it. There was a stairway beyond it.

"Sieb et il jif lou deré usti," he said.

He turned around and walked back to the engine. Zak looked at me and I nodded. He started heading up the staircase.

The room at the top was better furnished. There were mock martian artifacts displayed along the walls, paintings of the local landscape, and there were plants. Real plants. Two large monstera deliciosas at both ends of a red marble desk near the back wall. Two closed doors were past the desk.

"Houle!" I shouted.

One of the doors opened and a stout man came out. He was short. I would have confused him for a kid if it wasn't for the wrinkly mess that was his face. A Martian native- clearly familiar with its sun.

"Dib sir lous entrigedis. Setge, il entregou ist four ec," he said and walked towards the other door.

We followed him through a dark hallway. A door was at the end. He opened it. The walls in the room were painted light pink. There was a small bed in the corner. A few plushies on the shelves and a pile of toys on the floor.

"Nete oun iste?" He shouted into the empty room.

A small girl crawled out from under the bed.

"Lir, lir. Tie mi pirdiet." She said laughing.

"Netem is oure. Ils ti iever," he told her.

Her laugh faded.

"Ils mi iever?" She asked.

"Set." He turned to look at us and said, "Le seb qie ec. Les le selet tresi."

He headed back through the doorway, closing the door behind him.

Zak looked at me, "What the hell did we get ourselves into?"

"I don't know. I don't like it," I said.

The girl took a small backpack out from her bed and started putting her toys into it.

"Do we take her?" Zak asked.

"They don't seem to be hurting her. But she's clearly not theirs," I said.

"Nou feblou etglis," She told us with a mock-stern expression.

"Dou ti ieves?" Zak asked.

"Nou sí. Fir il jij det qie ale siri une prense," she said.

She smiled. The facade was clear. The poor thing was frightened. But it didn't seem to be of us.

"Let's just take her to the authorities," Zak said.

"What? Haven't you been to Ruife before?" I asked.

"No. I dated a girl from Tarre. She taught me Arcadian. All I know about Ruife is the usual stuff they teach in history class."

"The cops here are some of the most crooked you can find west of Saturn. They'll sell her organ harvesters without as much as a second thought. Or worse make her into a sex slave," I said.

"Fourfev ievet cou tet. Iea nou qarou ist soule," she said.

"She asked nicely," I said.

Zak shook his head, "Fine. But we're delivering her. She doesn't have papers and we're not exactly a group of caretakers."

"Vem cou nous," I told her.

She grabbed Zak's hand. He looked at me, asking for help. I shrugged and started walking towards the back exit.

"Coum ti iem's?" She asked Zak.

"Zak," he said.

"I tie?" She asked me.

"Liam. Qie tel ti?" I asked her.

"Sounie," she said.

"Qie bounet noum." I told her.

"Greca," she smiled.

"Don't get attached," Zak said.

We stepped out into a different street. I sent Tammy a message asking where they were. Tammy sent me her live location. Somehow, they'd found a bar.

"I'm just being nice. She's a kid," I said.

"A kid we have to deliver to potential crime lords. Don't get attached," he said.

"We shouldn't deliver her if they turn out to be crime lords." I said.

"We most definitely should. You want to steal their merchandise?" He asked.

"She's a kid," I said.

"There's a billion in the federation. Why does this one matter?" He asked.

"Because we can help this one," I said.

"What about the millions in refugee camps? Or the one's being sold into slavery? Or harvested for organs? You can't help them all."

"Yeah, I can't. But, if someone offers me a piece of gold I'm not going to deny it just because I can't have all the gold in the world," I said.

"I would if that piece of gold could lead to me being hunted down by a cartel," he said.

"The galaxy's large. They're not. If it is a cartel; I'm fine with never stepping foot in Arcadia again." I said.

"This isn't your home. I can't just scamper off to earth and never show my face again." He said.

"So, you'd let a child suffer?" I asked.

He hesitated.

"Yeah." He replied.

The bar was in sight.

"Wait here with her. I'll explain," I said.

"Why can't yo-" I ignored him and went into the bar.

"Liiiam!" Tammy shouted as soon as I stepped in.

They had a bucket of cerzis on the table and a bowl of buffalo wings.

"Like salt to water," I said.

"Didn't think we could do it?" She asked.

"I just didn't expect a bar in this type of neighborhood," I said and sat down.

"The cerzi's decent, wings are synthetic, about what you'd expect," Jeremy said.

I grabbed one and took a bite. The sauce didn't do a good job covering up the saline taste. Reluctantly, I swallowed and set the half-eaten wing down.

"They get Zak?" Tammy asked.

"I wish. He's outside with the 'package'. It's a bit... complicated," I said.

Tammy and Jeremy looked at each other.

"Complicated?" Jeremy asked.

"It's not exactly what we thought it'd be," I said.

"What is it?" Tammy asked.

I grabbed a cerzi out of the bucket and twisted the cap off.

"It's a kid. A girl, about 5 years old," I said and took a drink from the cerzi.

The excitement in their faces faded. Jeremy leaned back in his chair and Tammy crossed her arms. I finished my drink before either one said anything.

"What's her name?" Jeremy asked.

"Sounie. It means - I dreamt. Rather, she was someone's dream."

"What are we going to do with her?" Tammy asked.

"If they seem dangerous I don't think we should hand her over. Zak wants to deliver her, regardless."

"I'm with Zak. What are we going to do with a kid in the middle of a foreign planet?" Jeremy said.

"So you want to hand her over even if they'll take out her organs or make her into a sex slave?" I asked.

He took a moment to think before replying.

"We're in Arcadia. Yeah, it's not the best corner of the federation. But it's still federation land. As far as I'm aware- there's no pirate activity here. The cartels are pretty limited too. How likely are those scenarios?"

"I don't think we should hand her over," Tammy said.

"What?" We both asked.

"I- Well, she's a kid. Without a mom. We can't just hand an innocent kid over to some strangers."

"You want to sneak her on a ship and take her back to earth with you? Rescue a little Arcadian kid from mars and satisfy your earth-savior complex?" Jeremy asked.

"It's not that," she retorted, "On earth, or here, I can't let a kid suffer like that."

"Look, Jeremy's probably right. The chance that whoever we're supposed to deliver her to wants to harm her is small. We shouldn't just take an undocumented child earthside without knowing the whole situation." I said.

She rubbed her temples. "Fine. You're probably right. Just, we need to make sure these guys are safe. We need to talk to them and ask questions first."

"Delivery guys aren't supposed to be asking questions," Jeremy said.

"So what?" She asked.

"On the small chance it's a cartel- it makes us suspicious," he said.

"You said it's not likely. Let's see if your theory stands," I said, stood up, and started towards the door.

"Wait, we haven't paid," Tammy said.

"They don't use ether?" I asked.

"Nope. Only take eddies," Jeremy said.

"Wow. This place really nailed the 90's aesthetic," I said.

"So, kind of funny, we don't have any on us. You happen to?" Tammy asked.

"Yeah. But you owe me."

I took out my leather wallet and placed a couple of shiny beige-blue bills on the table.

"Wow, an antique. Can I take a look?" Jeremy asked as we started towards the door.

"Yeah," I handed him the wallet," Hand me down from my grandpa. He traveled the old world with this thing in his back pocket. Only fair that I continue the tradition."

"All my grandpa left me were a few crumbling asteroid mining companies and a lot of debt," Jeremy said.

"You got companies and you're complaining?" I asked.

"Typical for a rich boy. I never even meet mine," Tammy said.

"If I was rich I'd be somewhere far from here," Jeremy said.

"I said, rich boy. Not, rich man. Somehow you are way more

broke than I am." Tammy laughed.

"Bad rich boy habits?" I suggested.

"Yeah, we could say that," Jeremy said.

"Et vets les piremets in Elisiou?" Zak actually seemed interested in his conversation with Sounie.

"Set. Sou mes grende qie les qie tan e Tarre." There was a glimmer in his eye when he replied.

"Guooo, ispirou qie fande etr ien dá" Sounie said.

"Oufili set fandis. Firou met, ye vani. Illis sou Jeremy et Tammy," Zak said.

"Jeremy Tammy- Sounie," I said.

"Houle. Iris miet bounet," Sounie said.

"She says you're very pretty," Zak said.

"Thank you," Jeremy said.

"Tie nou. Iste miet piliedou fer sir bounet." Sounie laughed. Zak and I joined her.

"She said: Not you. You're too hairy to be pretty," I told him.

He genuinely looked hurt. "My beard is my best feature," he muttered to himself.

"Tell her I said thank you. And that she's very pretty too," Tammy said.

"Tammy detj greca. Et qie tie temban iris miet bounet," Zak said to Sounie.

Sounie was suddenly shy. "Greca," She said.

"We should go back to the hostel. Zak can babysit and we can get some more cerzis in us. I think they'll be essential for tonight," Jeremy said.

"I'd rather not be drunk for that," Tammy said.

"Me neither," I said.

"We could head to the center. We have 10 hours left until the delivery so we can kill time there," Zak said.

"You suggesting we spend the day babysitting?" Jeremy asked.

"I'm fine with that," Tammy said.

"I don't mind kids," I said.

"I do. Especially ones that call me hairy. I'll head back to the hostel. I met some guys last and they invited me for a drink this morning. Maybe they'll know something about whoever you went off with," Jeremy said.

"If you find out-let us know," I said.

"Will do. Okay, my Aventon will be here in less than a minute. He's picking me up at the end of the block. I'll see you guys later." He waved and started jogging towards his pickup spot.

"Ours is on the way. City center is only 20 minutes from here."

...

The worst part wasn't the dozens of sleepless nights. No, not the weeks spent having to constantly look around her shoulder. Not the outrageous amounts of money she'd spent on bribes. No, the worst part was that afternoon.

The girl had been handed off to the foreigners and it made everything so uncertain. Now, it was in the hands of complete strangers. She busied herself by double, and triple, checking everything. The weather generators were in order, no cop would be assigned anywhere near their district, they had the necessary drugs, and all the tools were in top condition.

She paced around the shop, wondering whether the foreigners would be stupid enough to go to the authorities. She had paid off officials, not the entire force. It was an extremelu concrete risk.

It wouldn't be unlikely for any normal citizen to report their suspicious activities. It'd happened the previous year. And they'd barely managed to hide that year's tribute. A local would have easily guessed the purpose for the delivery. Considering the date and tradition.

But foreigners were gullible. The idiots had probably thought they were getting drugs and ended up with live merchandise instead. But, it was a double-edged blade. They could be gullible enough to try and rescue her. She had eyes on them. But if they suddenly chose to take a cab to the port, there was little she could do.

And her whole world would shatter. It had persisted for more than a century. Every year, on the solstice. She'd participated in seven, and taken part in the festivities thirty-seven years. It was one of the few holidays her people celebrated. She understood the Terran's perspective on it, genuinely did. But she'd grown up with it and she had no regrets.

If her actions lead to the ritual's continuity breaking, she wouldn't be able to die peacefully. She would be remembered as the one who killed their traditions; instead of as the one who made assured that they wouldn't be forgotten.

..

"I still don't see anyone," Tammy said.

"It's not 00:03 yet," Zak said

"You think they're that specific about the pickup time?" I asked.

He shrugged and said nothing. Sounie was asleep in the back of a buggy we'd rented. Jeremy too, in the passenger seat. Tammy was pacing around the cemetery parking lot. Zak was sitting on the hood staring off into space.

We'd had a strangely enjoyable day with the Arcadian kid. Turns out our 'package' had an endearing personality. Still, it was stressful escorting an unregistered kid around a federation city. Getting her into the zoo had been an ordeal. We were tired and wanted the rest of our stay in Ruife to be realtively peacefull.

Tammy, on the other hand, didn't seem to tire of her own paranoia, "Its 01. C'mon. Being that specific is downright psychotic. Especially in Arcadia."

"Stop worrying about it. They're punctual. So what?" I asked.

"Who's that punctual in Ruife? You know how the Arcadian 'right now' really means 'an hour or two from now'? Who's this prompt in Arcadia but an international crime organization?"

"Oh, come on. You're making a lake out of a puddle," Zak said.

"Since when has timeliness made you a criminal?" I asked.

She didn't reply and continued pacing.

We were still the only ones at the cemetery at 00:02. It was an odd one, not just for Arcadia. Ruife's population had gone a bit crazy after earth stopped supplyign them, during the war. The food shortages led to desperate measures. Friends and family dying everyday, every preventitive measure being unsucessful. They were surviving but under extremely traumatizing conditions.

A few of the colonists were familiar with ancient religions. As a desperate measure, they decided to emulate them. Human sacrifice became commonplace. Manually reducing the colony's populatoin meant that resources were suddenly abundant to those who survived the rituals. The Native Arcadians failed to see the correalation and truly started to believe in the gods of earth's originary cultures.

With every country on Earth being at war, there was no one to stop them. The tradition spread from Ruife to the rest of Arcadia and a whole cult developed around a small Martian pantheon. They launched some odd, although intresting, building projects during, and after, the war period.

Temples to strange dieties. With altars at the top, from where they would carry out their rituals. Most of those building's were demolished to make way for the bustling federation city that was built during the last fifty years.

Most, not the one we were standing on. The Snake pyramid. Every year, on the winter solstice, the sun would hit it in such a way that a slithering shadow would make its way down the face of the structure. The outlaws claimed it was an old Martian god giving safe passage down into the underworld; safe passage for those sacrifced on the temple's steps.

For the Arcadians there was no heaven; only hell. All one could hope for in the afterlive was to secure a spot near the bottom of the levels of hell. The higher levels were said to be closer to mars. So, they were near the source of all human suffering. The lower levels were claimed to be the court of the king of hell. They weren't free of punishment, but existence there wasn't nearly as miserable as it was on the top levels.

Being sacrificed on the pyramid during the solstice was said to erase all of your sins. A a giant snake, who some claimed was the king himself, was said to carry the sould of the dead down to the lowest level. From there the king would judge them and assign them accordingly.

It's crazy stuff. I wasn't vaguely aware that human sacrifive had happened on Mars. But I had no clue how deep it went. I had nothing else to do while I waited and the pyramid really did seem like a place with an intresting history. Made out of Martian stone and still being one of the tallest buidlings in the whole city. The top is flat, with a altar in the center of the level plane and a cemetery sorrounding the altar. There's a few hundred tombstones, victims of the Martian mania.

Despite it's grandiosity, it's seldom visited. Tourists like to stay near the center. Sometimes they get frisky and go to the edge of the city, to take pictures of the pyramid. There's an air of mysticism about it.

Locals have a deep fear of the place. The Native tradition was wiped out as soon as the federation took the colony back. But some still believe it has an association with hell. When it became federation territory they renamed it, 'The Cemetery of our Lord and Savior Christ' and set up a bunch of catholic crosses and imagery in every corner of the cemetery. The next day it had disappeared.

The government said the few remaining Arcadians had been the purveyors of the vandalism. Three men were arrested and sent to the moons of Saturn. Urban myth says the spirits of those killed during the taking of the colony tore them out; the government simply needed a scapegoat for the missing structures.

The location was definitely a bit suspicious. But, if the child had no papers, it was the best place in Ruife to escape the government's watch.

A buggy's light lit up the parking lot shortly before 00:03. They parked on the opposite end of the lot and two men stepped out. They left the lights on. The glare hid their faces.

They walked towards us. Stopping a few meters away.

Exactly at 00:03 the taller of the two said, "Il peqant. Doun?"

Zak got up from the hood and moved next to me.

"Lou tinms. Fir, niesetms sebir fer qie lou qitirin." Zak said.

Tammy had stopped pacing. She was standing outside of the buggy's lights. They hadn't noticed her. She'd bought a translation pack at the tourism center and was, roughly, keeping up with the conversation.

"Sou les intrigedours. Nou is sie trebej seb," the other man said.

"Ban, qanrims seb," I said.

"Nou is esient di qanrim. Ist is ien dibir. Tan ien trebej et dios fet qie lou raletcin."

"Nou criou in dios intounc sie 'dibir 'mi veli. Coum ven e pinser qie setmplimint lis intrigerims iene nete eset noumes," Zak said.

The shorter one whispered something into the taller one's ear and he nodded.

Whithin a second they both had guns pointed at us.

"Dinousle," their tone was unequivocal.

Zak looked at me. He looked ready to faint, and he did. His sudden collapse provoked them and they shot the spot where he'd been standing. The bullet barely missed him.

Something struck the taller man and he went down. The shorter one shot the dark. The empty air sizzled. He shot again and missed.

He was distracted, still trying to hit the shadows. The other one had thrown his gun as he fell. It was only a few feet away from me. I quietly walked towards it and picked it up. Then I shot him in the thigh. He went down and tried shooting me. He hadn't bothered to aim and the shot wasn't even near me. A rock came from the shadow's and hit his gun hand. He cursed and recoiled in pain, accidentlaly throwing the gun a few feet from where he was. He started crawling towards it but Zak got the memo and kicked it away.

"What the hell was that?" Zal asked.

Tammy stepped out of the shadows.

"Not dangerous my ass," she said.

"Did you hit the first guy?" I asked.

She nodded.

"With what?!" Zak asked.

"Part of a gravestone, it was loose."

"Shit. That saved us," I said.

"You're welcome," Tammy said.

"Thank's," I said, absentmindedly. I was still trying to process the fact that I'd gotten shot at. Getting shot at was not on my bingo card when I left Earth.

At least the rounds weren't fatal. Although, they definitely left a mark. The wound on the guy I shot was nasty. Electric rounds. Zigzagging lines of burnt flesh extruded all around the missing part of his pant's leg. The smell was awful.

Somehow, Sounie was still sleeping.

"They're non-fatal," I said.

"They weren't trying to kill us?" Tammy asked.

"Wanted their merchandise with minimal police involvement," Zak said.

"What do we do now?" Tammy asked.

"Tie them up and question them?" I suggested.

Zak shrugged and Tammy nodded. I walked to the back of the buggy and took out the jumper cables. The shorter one was still squirming around. Tammy grabbed the gravestone and hit him over the head with it. I handed a cable to Zak and we got to work.

They were both unconsciouss so it wasn't difficult to tie wrap the cords around their arms and legs. Once we were certain they were secure, I grabbed one of the guns and set it to the lowest setting. I shot the taller one and he jerked up.

"Fuck off," he perked up.

"Ah, so you're not exactly a local are you?" I asked.

"I'm more of a local than any of those damn immigrants will ever be. Let us go or you'll have it bad," he tried to spit at me but the saliva landed on his shoe.

"Who are you?" I asked.

"None of your business," he said.

The gun was at set to 1, I switched it to 2 and shot his thigh.

"Fuck you," he grimaced.

I set it to 3 and pointed it at his crotch.

"You want to fuck so bad? How about we fix that?" I asked.

He stared at me, determined. I lightly pressed the trigger. The gun began to make a whirring sound. I could feel heat eminating from the barrel. He continued staring. I pressed harder and I started to feel the heat on my face. A few drops of sweat rand down his forhead.

"Okay. Fine," he hesitated, "My name's Riley. I'm from here; born on this wretched rock. Same as my father and granfather. You Terrans ain't have no business coming here and tying us up like this."

"What do you want the kid for?" I asked.

"Tribute," he stated.

"Tribute?" I asked.

"That's all I can say."

I set the dial to 4 and shot his other thigh.

"Shit!" He yelled. The stench of burnt flesh was revolting. I swallowed the bit of vomit that came up.

"Want to test the next setting? Wait-" I inspected the gun, "Wow, this thing can do plasma. That's not cheap."

"If I tell you I'll die anyways," he said.

"How come?" I asked.

"I'd kill myself. For betraying Arcadia," he said.

"Really? That strong of a nationalist?"

He seemed to think for a moment, "I would, or someone else eventually would. No one here would want to see me alive."

"Then sell this thing," I held the gun up, "You'd get enough for a one way ticket to Pluto or Saturn. Figure it out from there on."

He considered the offer, "Fine. I'm sure you'll kill me if I don't say anything so my life's on the line no matter what I do. I've always been intrested in what's out there. Why not fuck everything up before I find out?"

"Go on."

"She's tribute to the devil. Well, our interpretation of him. He saved us when all of your Terran gods left us to ruin. He blessed us, even. We owe our lives to him. So, we do what he demands."

"What do you mean by 'tribute'?" I asked.

"If you want it more bluntly: sacrifice."

"Human sacrifice?" I asked, shocked.

He nodded.

"I thought Arcadian's abandoned that tradition long ago."

He laughed, "World's not so simple. Pacts aren't broken that easily."

"Why a kid?" I asked.

"It's the winter solstice. It's our most important festival. We give him only the best tribute. A female, who has never given birth, and carries a certain kind of beauty," he said.

"It has to be a kid?" I asked.

"Not exactly. But she fits the description well. She was also born after her parents emigrated, it's a bonus."

"You're fucked," I said.

"May be. But our deal with Him has kept us alive till now," he shrugged.

"How do you know he's even real?"

"Look around you, you think we could have survived on this bastard without some sort of divine intervention? That's all the proof you need."

"Other colonies did just fine without killing kids," I said.

"They barely clung on to life while we prospered and grew large. Only Elysium rivaled us, before you illegal aliens started showing up. And we don't just sacrifice kids. Really, they're the exeption. This year's festival is meant to be a large one so we chose a tribute that was suting."

"You talk as if it's still going to happen," I said.

"It will," he said.

"What make's you feel so sure of that?" I asked.

"It has happened every year for over a century. Who are you to stop it? The devil will interven; the processions will proceed, despite our failure."

"And if they don't?"

"Then this city will be burnt to smithereens. If he doesn't have this sacrifice, his hunger will devour all of Ruife," he looked like wanted to add something. I waited.

"Honeslty, it wouldn't be the worst thing. At least then, we'll have had some form of revenge on you foreigners. So: let him. Let him feed on the sould of the city. It's been going to shit anyway. What time is it?"

I checked my watch.

"12:15," I said.

"You should get going then. Release me first, leave him," he nodded at his unconscious companion, "He'll try to stop you. Some more members should be showing up soon. The rituals supposed to start in a bit and her live should be taken at 1:06."

"Zak! Start the buggy!" I yelled and got up.

"Wait! You can't leave me," there was desperation in his voice.

This man was going to kill Sounie. Yet, something stopped me from just leaving him there. I set the plasma to the lowest setting. A thin ray of light burst out from the barrel of the gun. I cut the jumper cable.

"Here. Take this and get out of here," I said and handed him the gun.

"Can I get a ride?" He asked.

"No. You were about to kill the little girl that's in the back of the buggy. Find your own way out," I said and left him sitting on the ground.

"Floor it," I said as I closed the door.

The buggy lit the ground bellow it and gently rose up in the air. Then Zak floored it. We quickly went down the road that curved around the pyramid and connected to the main highway.

"What the fuck was that. We were supposed to hand her over not kill the guys," Jeremy said.

"We didn't kill them. Just... incapacitated," Tammy said.

"Whatever it was, that wasn't the plan," Jeremy said.

"Fuck the plan. They were going to kill her," I said.

"Are you sure about that?" Jeremy asked.

"Yes. I am. Our guy said a lot during our short chat. They're a fucking cult, okay? They were going to sacrifice her to some fabled martian deity." I said.

"Wait, we're dealing with the Arcadian cult?" Zak asked.

"The cult?" Tammy asked.

"Everyone on Mars knows about them. But, I thought it was history. I didn't know they still existed," Zak said.

As we were connecting to the highway, a buggy passed us, heding up to the pyramid.

"Who are they?" Tammy asked.

"It's a long story. The Arcadians developed their own religino during the war period. It's really intresting, the whole philosophy behind it, but part of their tradition is human sacrifice," Zak said.

"You're joking, right?" Tammy asked.

"He's not," I said.

"What the actual fuck," her eyes showed a touch of fear.

"Fucking great. Should have read up a bit before I got on that damn shuttle," Jeremy said.

"Would have helped," I said.

The highway was mostly empty. Our bickering woke Sounie up.

"Si piedin caler?" She asked.

"Great. Now the kid's up," Jeremy said.

"It's your yelling that woke her up," Tammy said.

"I wasn't yelling."

"Totally were."

"You're all being loud. What the hell do we do with her now?" Zak asked.

"Has anyone considered that she could have parents?" It seemed so stupidly obvious once I asked the question.

"I hadn't thought about that..." Tammy said.

"Sounie, tanis ien pep et mam?" Zak asked.

She nodded. We all stayed silent for a moment.

"Why hadn't one of you already asked?" Jeremy said.

"I kind of just assumed she was an orphan" I said. I hadn't even consdiered the possibility of her being kidnapped.

"We could have saved ourselves from this whole mes-"

"Dound vetv ties peis?" Zak asked Sounie.

"341 B, padres roujes."

"Bloody hell," Zak said.

"What?" Tammy asked.

"Her parent's are here, in Ruife."

No one said anythign after that. Zak put the adress into the navigator and we were there within twenty minutes.

Her parent's lived on the outskirts of the city. They managed a lakeside resort. We had knock a few times before they woke up and opened the door. But, once they did, they were ecstatic. We explained the situation to Sounie's father while her mom put her down for bed.

We agreed to contact the authorities in the morning and they let us stay at one of the lakeside houses. It wasn't peak season so most of them were empty.

It was dark when I woke up. It was 11 am. Rogue storms on Mars are rare. The federation has the climate locked down well. If they want the wind to blow west at 4km per hour- it will. If they want no wind for 3 months straight (perfect during the tourist season)- there won't be any wind.

There was no other explanation for the climate but a storm. Muddled purple-grey clouds filled the horizon. A faint ember barely shone through. It was cold, even for Mars.

The lakes were deserted. I remembered seeing other buggys in the parking lot the previous night. It was empty when I went to ask Sounie's parent's for a coffeemaker. The one in our kitchen was broken.

"Odd weather." I said to her dad while he looked for the coffeemaker.

"Terrifying. I've lived here since I was 5 and have never seen anything like it. Ah, here we go." He took out the coffeemaker and placed it on kitchen table.

"Any clues as to the cause?" I asked.

"Its likely tied to the cult," he said, sternly.

"You think so?" I asked.

"They do somethign every year. I- I was never sure if the rumours were true until you lot came last night. Last year they launched fireworks at two am, the year before that they used giant speakers to wake the whole city up."

"So it's not like they do it secretely?" I asked.

"No. They want the whole city to know. They want the federation to know. But most people think they're just seperationist trying to make a scene. But our Sounie, god she was-" he started crying. I comforted him but left as soon as it was appropriate.

"Get any food?" Tammy asked as soon as I was through the door.

"No, I was going to ask but her dad started bawling so it didn't feel appropriate. I think there's a gas station 10 minutes from here," I said.

"I'll go." Jeremy grabbed the keys, which were on the kitchen countertop, and eagerly left the house.

"Think he'll come back?" Tammy asked.

"Probably not," Zak said.

"Guy at the front desk said that this weather's caused by a 'certain martian cult'."

"No shit?" Tammy asked.

"Yeah. Aparently they make a big scene every year."

I turned the coffee maker on and poured myself a cup. The weather had gotten worse. The wind had kicked up a thin layer of red dust. Thin rays of light made the rusted soil glimmer. The world was a mix of indigo, deep grey, and red. The ring around the the sun glowed purple.

I thought I saw something moving through the clouds. Then I blinked and it was gone. I had no idea how they were pulling it off. But it was defintely impressive.

The door burst open.

"Fuck. Okay. I did what you asked. Get that thing out of my

face," Jeremy's voice.

I turned around and the Arcadian guy from the warehouse was holding him at gunpoint. He hit the back of Jeremey's head with the gun and threw him in to the living room. Jeremy staggered but managed to catch himself. He stood up. His face was full of guilt.

"Sorry. They had a gun pointed at me, I didn't have an option."

The gun was on the kitchen counter. I reached for it but the Arcadian was a quick shot. The thing blew into a dozen pieces before my hand reached the hilt.

"Come on. All 'f you. Go out." He was hard to understand through the thick accent. We stayed still, staring blankly.

"Endin. Nou tingou tampou fer ist." His tone was clear. Him beckoning with the gun was clearer. We all left the house.

"I told you where they were! I thought we had an agreement!" We heard Jeremy yell from inside.

"Deal through. You come too." The Arcadian said.

"I'm not going with you."

"Dimesadous proublims," the Arcadian muttered to himself.

The air sizzled then there was the sound of a body hitting the floor.

The buggy we'd seen in the shop had been fixed. It was a big one. 10 seater, clearly made for treks in to the marscape. I sat in the second row. 'My' guy was in the other seat. Bruised, bloody, tied up, and unconscious. The Arcadian got in to the passengers seat, there was another one of them at the driver's seat.

I looked behind me. I realized Sounnie was sitting next to Tammy. She was crying softly. I hadn't heard any shots so I assumed her parent's were fine. Probably unconcsious, but alive. Zak was in the 4th row, next to yet another cultist.

I started, "I don't think we ca-"

"No talk." The Arcadian said and shot me with a non-fatal round.

..

We were in the cemetery parking lot when I regained consciousness. The front row was empty and I couldn't see the cultist anywhere. Barring the one sitting next to Zak- holding a heavy rifle.

"You gonna shoot me too?" I asked.

There was no reply. I looked behind me. He shrugged and then yawned.

"Guess he doesn't get payed enough to care." I said.

"How was your nap?" Zak asked.

"Refreshing." I said.

Tammy started crying.

"Nou ti esiests. Noumes mi qitirin e met. Nou e tet." Sounie said and patted her forearm.

The tears didn't stop.

"Qie ven e fec coun nous?" I asked the cultist.

He shrugged again and continued staring out the window. I stared and he ignored me. Then he perked up. He didn't say anything for a few seconds. Merely nodded and gave grunts of agreement.

"Get out." He said.

I tried the door.

"It's locked." I said.

"Use the other one." He replied and stepped out of the buggy.

"Excuse me." I said to 'my' guy as I opened his door and stepped over him.

It was freezing. The lights of the city sparkled the way a city's lights sparkle in winter. Which was eerily uncanny when juxtaposed with the martian landscape (and the progressively worsening storm clouds).

He pointed with his rifle and I followed. I lead the line and he took the back. The destination was clear.

The tip of the pyramid jutted out from the center of the cemetery. I'd seen it on tourism websites but it was stranger in real life. It was a pyramid in of itself. Some 15 meters tall with 4 columns and a martian marble roof at the top.

They were lit with a neon green light that seemed to

emanate from their cores. I had no choice but to walk straight the the ritual-place.

The two cultist were waiting at the base of the mini-temple. They were naked. Butt naked. Scars lined their thighs and torsos. They weren't plain scars. They said things. Prose started at the base of their necks and ended at their knees. Passages made with careful incisions. Words payed for with blood.

I stopped a few meters away from them.

"Keep going." The one with the rifle said.

I hesitated.

"Don't kill her." Tammy said.

"It's not a choice. Tribute must be given." He said.

"Don't kill her. Kill me." She said.

I turned around to look at the exchange.

"You?" He asked.

She was still holding Sonie's hand.

"You want a whore's daughter, right?" She asked.

"Well, that's one of the requirements. She's gotta be beautiful, impregnable, and never have married." He replied.

"My mom was one of the best New Orleans whores there was. Slut her whole life. Fucked every guy on her college football team then dropped out to strip for a living. Never met my dad. Don't think she had a single clue who he was. I'd say I'm more than gorgeous, definitely pregnable, and have never even been proposed to." She said.

"Tammy, don't." Zak said.

"I have to. It's not much of a choice." She said.

He started mumbling to himself. I turned around and saw that the other guys were mumbling to themselves too.

"Step forward." He said.

"Take her." She handed Sounie's hand to Zak. He grabbed it.

She stepped forward. One of the cultists had a large III scarred on the middle of his chest. The other had an O. The one with the III grabbed Tammy and kissed her. She pushed back but he grabbed a fistful of hair and pulled her forward. She let out a cry and stopped resisting.

He let go and she fell down.

Sounie started sobbing quietly. She closed her eyes and hugged Zak's leg. Burying her head in it.

"She'll do. Get her ready." He said to the one with the O.

Tammy'd been put in to some sort of trance. There was nothing we could do. They stripped her clothes off and threw them to the ground.

"Sieb erret." The one with the O commanded.

She started walking up the stairs. I could see why Liam had stuck around. Her figure didn't leave much to be desired. Her gait seemed more feminine (than usual) as she walked up the steps. The way everything swayed was alluring.

As soon as she was halfway up the stairs the sky suddenly burst alive. Rays of lighting moved thorughout the clouds in a strangely organized way. There were thousands of individual ones yet they seemed to move in unison. I didn't want to admit to myself what it looked like. But the way they moved through the clouds was far too reminiscent of the rattle snakes I used to catch with my brother when we were kids.

It glowed brighter with every step she took. Then she was at the top. I hadn't even noticed the cultist go up but he was there, waiting for her.

She lay down on a stone table.

I wanted to look away. For some reason- I couldn't.

He took out a long, black knife. The lighting reflected off the glossy surface. Making it look as if it were trapped within the knife.

She gained a moment of lucidity and cried out.

Then he stabbed her. She screamed.

Not in the heart- in the stomach. Right where I imagined her uterus would be.

Painful sobs were escaping her lips.

He took the knife out, partly. Then he dragged it up to her chest, cutting a line through the skin in between.

She screamed. I saw her lips move, her body react. But I didn't hear it.

The crackling of the lighting was deafening. It sounded like laughter. Some corrupted, distorted, audio recording played on a bad speaker.

The other cultist had appeared and was holding her arms down. Her legs were kicking empty air.

He peeled the skin away. I couldn't even blink. My eyes were glued. I could hear Zak sobbing beside me. But my view was glued on the unfolding ritual.

He reached in between her rib cage and she shook uncontrollably. Then nothing.

Her legs fell down and hit the stone table.

The other pulled her ribs apart and he took out the heart.

They were laughing. Faces full of excitement.

He took a bite from the heart and handed it to his friend. He licked it like a child enjoying a popsicle on a summer day.

Then he tore in to it. Only one bite but he clearly savored it.

Then lighting struck and I went blind.

White, searing, hot.

The heat faded but I still only saw white.

The crackling was gone and Sounie and Zak were crying.

After the burning sensation faded- I realized tears were rolling down my cheeks too.

I was out of the trance and I collapsed on the marble floor.

We didn't say anything.

After a few minutes I started to regain my sight.

The cultist were gone. So were the clouds.

It was a fair Martian morning. Same as many others.

But we weren't. We, certainly, weren't.

"Did Sounie see?" I asked Zak after I'd had time to slightly process what had happened.

"No. I don't think she saw anything. Her head was stuck to my leg the entire time." He said.

"Did you?" I asked.

His silence said everything I needed to know.

"I couldn't look away." I said.

"I tried. With every fibre of my being, I tried." He replied.

"What about her?" I asked.

"I think she wanted me to take care of her." He said.

"Are you going to?" I asked.

"I think I owe her that." He said.

"Sounie kind of reminds me of her. When she was a kid. I think she noticed that too." I said.

"You knew her then?" He asked.

"Yeah. We hav- we had a long history." I said.

"Shit. I'm sorry." He said.

I stood up.

"This isn't an 'I'm sorry' kind of situation. But, 'shit' is appropriate." I said.

"'Shit' describes this whole day." He said.

"I'll put it in my diary. I think I'll be getting a ticket on the first shuttle out of Mars. A vacation somewhere tropical is warranted. Maybe I'll go to Neo New Orleans, as a tribute." I said.

"I've gotta get her to New London. Explain this whole mess to my family. Fuck know's if they'll believe me." He said.

"Yeah. Good luck with that. Take care of her." I said.

"Thanks. I'll do what I can." He lay down on the marble floor and sighed. Sounie was still sobbing, quietly.

"Well, till some other time." I said.

"Till some other star." He replied.

I walked towards the exit and didn't bother to look back. It was a Martian morning like any other. But I was permanently changed. The world had changed- or at least my view of it- and there would never be another morning like yesterday's.

PURSUIT OF FLOWERS
- TEASER

This short story collection was written after I began working on Pursuit of Flowers. It is also being published before the novel's release. So, here's a short teaser of my upcoming supernatural horror novel:

Chapter 8 - The Devil Went Down to Cannalt

He stepped off the asphalt and started pedaling. Immediatly, he felt light, the wind swifter. An experience akin to flying, he reckoned; the effects of the joint.

Immense pines lined both sides of the asphalt. The sun had almost set. Shadows filled the forest.

There was a dip in the road ahead. He leaned into the frame of the bike and let gravity take him full speed. He went from 15mph to 30mph. He leveled out to 25mph as the road straightened again. Then he saw it.

Almost like it materialzed directly in his path of motion. He didn't have time to stop. The feeling was awful. Like hitting a spongy wall of mist with a few hard bones in between. He flew off his bike. The collision launched him straight towards a jagged pine stump.

He lay on the ground for a few seconds. He tried getting up but quickly went back down. He lay still for a bit. His left ankle was slightly twisted but the pain wasn't horrible. He managed to get up, using his right arm to pull himself up with the help of the stump.

His left arm felt awful. It'd taken the brute of the impact. It was torn up in multiple spots. Splinters and dirt filled the skin-deep wounds. The pain in his ankle quickly subsided. He was able to walk with only a slight limp.

Whatever he'd hit was gone. There was a red streak which led across the road in to the other side of the woods. It was dotted with tufts of grey-brown fur.

He was relieved, after chicking his bike, to see that everything was fine. The only casualty, besides himself, had been his phone's screen protector. He tore the cracked glass off the screen and stuck it in his pocket. He carefully got back on to the bike, making sure not to hit his ankle on the metal.

The pain started to fade. Endorphins already cursing their way through his body.

This is going to suck tomorrow.

The somber light of early moonrise put the forest under a muddled shadow. He hurried home as the evening let go of its last hold on the day.

He was nearing the edge of town. He moved onto the sidewalk. Occasional streetlights lit the path. A passing car caught his attention and he glanced towards the road. Then he caught sight of the red. His arm was painted with it. It struck him strange how normal it felt.

He took a right turn at a four way stop that lay at the entrance to civilization. A few three story apartment buildings broke the monotony of the suburban landscape. He got to the end of the development and left his bike on the driveway.

The lights were off. He didn't bother turning them on and them and headed to the bathroom in the dark.

He looked like he was the one that'd been hit. There was a large gash on his forehead, above his right eye, that he hadn't noticed earlier. Tons of other small infractions dotted his body. A scrape above his lip. A gash below his knee. Slowly, the pain was starting to seep in.

He couldn't ignore it any longer. He lifted his left arm up to the mirror. A shiver coursed through his body. Slivers of sharpened pine wood, the largest about 6 inches in length, were lodged all throughout his forearm.

Clint turned the shower on and let the water warm up for a few seconds, while he studied it further. He touched it. The mix of blood, dirt, and wood shavings had created a grainy goo that felt awful.

Fuck.

Small pockets of steam were starting to emanate from the shower floor. He placed his arm under the running water.

"Fuck," he whimpered.

Tears came as he waited for the water to carry off all the dirt and shavings. It seeped deep into the dozens of tiny scrapes. Every severed nerve reactivated. He turned the water off.

Flesh blood quickly started to cover his arm again. He heard a door open.

"Clint?" Meg knocked on the bathroom door.

He managed a painful, "What's up?"

"Are you okay?" She asked.

"Yup, perfectly fine," Clint said, his voice was clearly strained.

He heard her footspets retreat into the living room, then the quiet click of the lightswitch. She didn't say anything, then she walked back to the bathroom door.

"Why are you bleeding?" She asked.

"I'll answer if you get the first aid kit," he said.

"It was your bike, right?" She asked.

"Could you just get the first aid kit?" He asked.

She left and came back a few seconds later. He opened the bathroom door. A trail of blood had followed Clint, almost making a cross on the floor. There was blood all over the sink, as well.

"Clint! What the hell?" Meg said.

"It wasn't my fault," he stammered.

"Clint! I told you this was going to happen," she said.

She made her way into the bathroom, avoiding the slippery bits of the floor. She grabbed his wrist and quickly lifted his hand up. He tried not to show the pain.

"My god," she shook her head.

She set the first aid kit down on the small space between the round hanging sink and the mirror.

"Wait," she said as she ran back out.

"Meg!" He called after her.

She came back with a humidifier and some small bottles.

"Meg I told you that stuff doesn't work," he managed.

"Shut up," she said

She quickly plugged the device into the outlet and put it on the windowsill. She filled it with water and a concoction of oils from the bottles. She opened the first aid box and took out some pill bottles, bandages, and a set of tweezers.

She held up a bottle of pills, "I wouldn't take these. But, they're great for pain. So, its u-"

He held his good hand out. She shook two pills onto his palm. He looked up at her.

"Really?" She asked.

He didn't advert his gaze. She shook out 3 more. He swallowed them dry. The room started to fill with the aroma of lavender, chamomile, and a hint of rosemary.

"At least they smell nice," Clint said.

"See," she said.

She beckoned towards the toilet. He sat down.

"Doesn't change the fact that it's total crap," he said.

"Whatever," Meg said.

She held her hand out. He extended his arm towards it. She grabbed his wrist and twisted it. Exposing his lower forearm. She winced.

"What the hell, dude," she said as she pulled out one of the smaller splinters.

"I hit a coyote," he said.

"What?!" She stopped and looked at him.

"I hit a coyote. Fast. It threw me off and I hit a stump. It was all pointy." He said.

She looked back down.

"I can tell," she murmured.

He let out a small gasp as she pulled out a 3 inch splinter.

.

The effect of the pills faded as he'd started to fall asleep. The pain grew until he couldn't bare it. He stood up and opened his backpack. He still had one joint left from Oscar's party. He'd been planning on saving it for after practice but his needs were more immediate. He went to his closet and took out a glass pipe, a box of matches, and a bottle of water.

Clint snuck past Meg, who'd fallen asleep on the couch (watching a late night soap opera), and went out in to the yard.

He unrolled the tip of the joint under the moonling. He held it between his forefinger and thumb, flipped it upside down (with the tip resting on the glass bowl), and pinched it.

The loose weed fell out in sporadic bursts. Some fell on the table. With a bit of effort, he scooped it up with his good hand and put it in the bowl. He stopped once it was half full.

He set the joint down and picked up the matchbox. He struck it and it lit. He set the matchbox down and picked up the pipe.

He brought the pipe up to his lips. The flame danced around the sides of the glass bowl as he took in the hit. He started coughing immediately. The smoke that escaped his lungs was murky yellow. He grabbed the water bottle and took a large drink. He tried swirling it around but the urge to cough was too large and he spat it out.

He couldn't get the rotten, coppery, taste out. Most of the bowl was unlit. He grabbed his phone and turned the flashlight on.

The weed was red.

He touched it. It was moist. He looked down at his hand. The bandage was hanging off. His palm was bleeding.

He heard a rustling beyond the backyard. He looked up, the glow of the moon didn't reveal anything. He ignored the rustling and went back to his hand. He grabbed the water bottle, tilted it, and let the water slowly trickle down the wound. There were nuggets of weed inside the gash. He placed the phone at the edge of the coffee table and turned on the light. He heard more rustling coming beyond the fence. He ignored it and slowly started picking them out.

Once it looked clean he rewrapped the bandage around his palm. He grabbed the joint and started to roll weed onto the bowl again. This time he checked it. There was no blood. But, there were a few loose strands of fur in it. He looked at the sleeve of his hoodie and saw that whatever he'd struck had likely been shedding. He pinched it with his fingers and threw it out in to the wind.

His eyes reflected the golden glow of the burning match-head. He finished the bowl in one hit.

He stood up. The rustling grew louder. He quickly picked his phone up and shone the light at the fence. The shadows of the wire backyard fence spread across the barren lot beyond. He moved the light around. The rustling was gone. He turned the light off and took a few steps towards the entrance.

Then he heard the gate that led in to the drive way creak. He turned.

A canine was at the entrance to the yard. Its hind legs were disturbingly wrong. Slender and far too long. Its head rested slightly lower than its tail. It was dripping with blood. Tufts of fur were missing all throughout its right side. The exposed flesh gleamed in the twilight.

Clint froze. The creature edged closer, silently. He started walking backwards, towards the fence. The canine stopped and followed his movement. It edged closer once he stopped at the corner. Clint was immobile. It sat down on its abnormally long hind legs a few feet from where Clint was planted. He heard its voice in his head.

-Heal me,- it felt like a thought. But it wasn't his own.

Clint tried backing away further but he hit the fence post. The shock traveled up his arm. The pain was immense.

-I can get rid of that for you. But I need your aid first,- the creature thought.

-What the hell were in those pills," Clint muttered to himself.

-I'm no hallucination,- it said.

It started walking closer towards Clint. He tried backing away again but this time he hit his swollen ankle on the post and the pain drove him to the ground. His back leaned against the post and his legs splayed out in front of him. He could see it better from the new angle. The proximity helped.

The coat was mostly grey but a brown smudge started at at the base of its tail and spread all the way to the head. It grew a lighter shade as it went up the creature's body. It's jaw a soft white. Snout dry-grass yellow.

It looked like a coyote. It had the lean quality, the ears, the face. But the proportions were all wrong. It pushed its snout against his ankle. The pain rekindled.

-See.

"What the hell," Clint said quietly.

-You ran me over. That could have been that. I could have simply cursed you and been on my way.

"You're what I hit?" He asked with disbelief.

-Who you hit. Our paths didn't have to cross again. Tell me then; why did you summon me?

"Summon you?" Clint asked.

-You mixed your blood with coyote hair, and then smoked it. That is how I'm summoned,- it stated.

"I- I didn't know. It was an accident," Clint said.

-There's are no such things.

"You ran out of the woods. I didn't even se-"

-You saw perfectly fine. You choose to go faster.

"I-"

-Quiet. You hit me. Then summoned me. You have no choice but to help me.

"What happens if I don't?" Clint asked nervously.

It barred its teeth.

The way its mouth curled made it seem as if it was smiling.

"Want to find out?" It asked.